"Y

Keane looked out at the empty field, then added, "Just like the first time."

Gypsy stood rigid. Overhead a star shot from the sky, curving in a swift arc to who knew where.

"How poetic," Keane muttered. "She even generates her own special effects." He came up behind her and gently touched her hair.

"Gypsy." He said it tentatively. "Look, I'm sorry, but—"

"Maybe I deserve it," she murmured.

"Maybe you do." Keane steeled himself and turned her to face him.

She didn't bother to hide her tears. She merely gazed at him as he moved closer and took her into his arms.

"You're as alive as I am, right here and right now. Let me prove it to you. . . ."

Deanna Lindon

Deanna Lindon began her career as an actress and amateur filmmaker, but soon discovered that writing offered a wider freedom of expression.

She is single and lives in Phoenix, Arizona, with her two Siamese cats, Banshee and Pixie. When not keeping these spirited mother and daughter cats in line, she can be found hard at work on her next novel.

Dear Reader:

Romance is handled with a light touch by this month's witty and insightful authors. Courtney Ryan, author of *Cody's Gypsy* (#438) which so many of you loved, has outdone herself—again—in *Ten to Midnight* (#468). And for skilled new Second Chance at Love author Deanna Lindon, not even the sky's the limit in *Air Dancer* (#469).

It's amazing, but true. In *Ten to Midnight* (#468), Courtney Ryan has crafted a plot, hero, and heroine as entertaining as her many others over the years. When Stevie Knight, the owner of—and force behind—a company that specializes in unforgettable events, is hired to kidnap a groom-to-be, it's just another day at the office for her. So when her partner delivers a blindfolded and bewildered M. J. Connover to Stevie's limo, she takes off for the bachelor party that awaits. Another mission accomplished it seems, but Stevie doesn't realize she has the wrong Connover. Happily a hostage of the seductive voice and entertaining antics of his kidnapper, Mick doesn't say a thing. If only he could see the face behind the voice, and the mouth that surprises him with a good-bye kiss before he's dumped on the corner. Though she does her best to remain undiscovered, Stevie inevitably surrenders to Mick's disarming ways. But there's still one hurdle Stevie has to overcome before she'll be Mick's willing captive forever...

Gypsy Gallagher is an adventurous soul whose truly happy moments are those she spends airborne. An acknowledged flying ace, clear weather and a free schedule are her only requisites for the perfect day. Of course, her life hasn't always been that simple. But tragedy's place is in the past; Gypsy is more interested in the future. Big-time journalist Keane McCready is interested in the future, too—ideally a future with Gypsy. Assigned to cover her for his magazine, Keane is taken with this fiery spirit full of surprises. Gypsy's only interest, however, is in getting rid of him. Not only does Keane stir disturbing images of the past, he's wreaking havoc on the present. She refuses to be grounded by any man, this handsome reporter included. But Keane's determined to exorcise the past and eliminate the barrier that keeps him from his *Air Dancer* (#469).

Also from Berkley this month is new author Teresa Medeiros. In *Lady of Conquest*, we're taken back to ancient Ireland and the time of the Fianna, led by Conn of the Hundred Battles and Gelina Ò Monaghan, who wields a sword called Vengeance. Despoiler of Gelina's family, Conn takes her in when she has no one. Not yet a woman, Gelina still is able to stand alone against Ireland's mightiest warriors; she has a will of steel until it is weakened by her passion for the one man she hates most. Their forbidden love becomes a personal war fought with swords and embraces, promises and betrayal. In the tradition of *Lion of Ireland*, *Lady of Conquest* is a beautifully written historical novel that will stay with you for a long time to come...

The sizzling *New York Times* bestseller, *The Duchess of Windsor* by Charles Higham, is now a Charter paperback. The world has held the Duchess of Windsor—Mrs. Wallis Simpson—in endless fascination. But until now, the world hasn't heard much of what there is to know. Her power over Edward VIII, who gave up his throne for her . . . her fairy-tale rise to royalty . . . her ruthless power schemes . . . her unique seductive bedroom practices . . . her notorious Nazi connections. Fully documented from exclusive sources, *The Duchess of Windsor* unveils the secret life of one of the most talked-about women of the century. "Fascinating!" *USA Today.* "A shocker!" *Cosmopolitan.* Don't miss it!

Wildflower, by Jill Marie Landis, author of the spectacular novel *Sunflower*, is truly a fabulous read. Meet Dani, a spirited beauty, who, dressed as a man, dupes unwanted attackers and survives the untamed Rocky Mountain wilderness of 1830. But her heart holds passionate dreams and unspoken desires. And meet Troy, a darkly handsome explorer who kidnaps Dani on a lark, and is himself captivated by her beauty and unwavering spirit. From the great peaks of the West to the lush seclusion of a Caribbean jungle, Dani and Troy discover the deepest treasures of the heart.

August is a great month for romance. I can almost promise you September will be even better! Until then, happy reading!

Hillary Cige

Hillary Cige, Editor
SECOND CHANCE AT LOVE
The Berkley Publishing Group
200 Madison Avenue
New York, NY 10016

DEANNA LINDON
AIR DANCER

BERKLEY BOOKS, NEW YORK

To Pat

CHAPTER
One

SOMETHING WAS WRONG WITH the biplane's engine.

Gypsy Gallagher cocked her auburn head and listened. The vintage aircraft had completed its aerobatic display for the annual Oshkosh, Wisconsin, air show, and was on its way in. Gypsy, having already performed, stood with a mechanic outside one of the field's hangars, anxiously watching the red-and-white Stearman.

"What do you think, Tim?" she asked as a thread of tension wove through her body.

"Sounds like an air lock in the fuel line," he replied, shading his eyes against the afternoon sun. "He's coming in way too low. I don't like the looks of this."

Gypsy nodded. Even from the ground the telltale sputtering was evident to her pilot's ear. Overhead, the Red Devils swung into their spectacular bomb-burst maneuver, commanding the full attention of the two hundred thousand–plus crowd that had gathered for the largest air convention in the world.

On display at Wittman Field were fifteen thousand vintage and experimental aircraft of every size, shape, and color imaginable. The July sky was cloud-free and vivid blue on the eighth and last day of the show. An air of festivity permeated everyone and everything. No one paid any mind to the troubled Stearman.

It was indeed coming in too low. Gypsy was aware of the danger involved, and her dread grew. The engine could stall completely. "Come on, come on," she groaned, willing the pilot to pull back on the stick. "Who's flying her?"

"Dick Russell," Tim answered. "Seventy-two-year-old veteran of one too many air shows." He frowned. "If he has any trouble landing that thing we have a double problem."

Gypsy took her eyes off the biplane for a split second. "What are you talking about?"

"If you hobnobbed more with the other pilots, you'd know there's been a journalist from *World View* magazine poking around here all week, asking for rides. Russell must've given in."

"You mean he's carrying a passenger? Oh, my God." Gypsy squinted to get a better look at the two-seater. Sure enough, there was someone in the forward cockpit. She clenched her hands into fists. Stunt maneuvers were risky enough for the most experienced of pilots, and insurance premiums were outrageous. To take an uninsured passenger up for this kind of flying was beyond stupidity.

The sputter grew louder as the craft neared the edge of the runway. Then, as if some invisible hand had pulled a plug, there was total silence. Dick Russell would have to make a dead-stick landing, and he had only a few seconds in which to do it.

Gypsy tensed. Five years earlier she'd been witness to a similar emergency, only that time it had ended in tragedy. At twenty-five she'd felt her world crumble, and now at thirty she remembered all too vividly the flames and the smell of leaking fuel.

The Stearman, its nose pointed downward, glided to the pavement, then struck with sudden force, blowing both tires of the landing gear and slewing sideways to a 180-degree angle.

Before it came to a complete stop Gypsy was running, her long-legged stride covering the distance in seconds. The bottom-left wing and part of the top wing of the plane had crumpled, allowing fuel to escape. It rested on its side, still as death.

Tim was already tending to the pilot, so Gypsy focused her efforts on the man in the forward seat. He sat, goggles askew, in shock but with no injuries that she could see.

"Are you hurt?" she yelled over the sound of approaching sirens.

After a moment's hesitation he shook his head.

"Then help me unbuckle this so you can get out of there, unless you want us both to burn to a crisp." Gypsy spoke with harsh urgency, her hands moving over the man's safety harness as he fumbled to respond.

His eyes followed hers to the dripping gas, and the sight broke his trance. Galvanized, he finished unbuckling himself and leaped over the side of the plane. Gypsy took his arm and they ran, only a few yards behind Tim and the limping pilot.

Seconds later they heard a *whoosh* behind them and felt the heat. Before Gypsy knew what hit her the man grabbed her about the waist and threw her to the ground, landing on top of her with enough force to knock the breath from her lungs.

They were chest to chest, and Gypsy felt the hard

strength of his body on hers as she struggled to draw in air. She tried to move but he was like a rock, his own breath warm on her cheek. Slowly it dawned on her what he was attempting to do. He was trying to protect her, shielding her body with his as he waited for who knew what.

When nothing came he raised his head in confusion, then reached up to remove his goggles.

Gypsy found herself looking into a pair of eyes as blue as the sky above her. At close range she could see the fine lines that fanned out from the corners onto an interesting, dust-covered face. "Will you let me up?" she gasped, trying to ignore the way her breasts flattened against him with every feeble breath she took. It was difficult, if not impossible.

He blinked once but didn't move. Then he glanced behind them and realized the plane had merely caught fire, not blown into a million pieces. "I...I'm sorry," he mumbled, and shifted his weight so that he sat on the grass beside her. He ran a hand through his mussed, golden-brown hair. "I thought—uh, never mind...just...I'm sorry."

Gypsy slowly got to her feet and brushed off her flight suit. Adrenaline still coursed through her and she began to shake in its wake. "Do you know what an idiotic stunt that was?" she asked, voice deadly flat.

He stared up at her. "Look, I didn't mean to hurt you—"

"Not that!" She gestured toward the burning biplane, heedless of the activity around them as the emergency equipment arrived and the crew concentrated on putting out the fire. "You could have been killed. You were damned lucky you weren't seriously injured, do you under*stand*? When I get my hands on Dick Russell for agreeing to give you a joy ride, he'll never fly again. Both of you behaved so irresponsibly it disgusts me!"

The man's eyes widened. Standing, he brushed off his own borrowed flight suit. "Hey, wait a minute," he began.

"No, you wait a minute," she continued, unable to stop now that she'd gotten started. She needed to lash out, to hurt him for that split second of horror he'd unknowingly inflicted on her. "The EAA is going to hear about this, and I am personally going to see to it you're banned from this field."

"The Experimental Aircraft Association knows I'm here, lady," he shot back, indignant. "If you don't believe me you can check it out yourself. I had every right to be up there."

"The hell you did!" Gypsy's comment was all but drowned out by the increasing pandemonium. Curious onlookers poured onto the field, and the emergency crew had its hands full keeping them back from the crash site. Tim talked to two EAA officials off to their left.

The Stearman's passenger seemed oblivious to everything but Gypsy. "Look," he said. "My name is Keane McCready, and I was sent here to do a story on Oshkosh by *World View* magazine. I've already been cleared by the EAA."

"To fly?"

"Yes!"

"In the show itself?" When he hesitated an instant too long Gypsy nodded. "I thought not." Tim motioned for her to join him and she turned to go, but McCready took hold of her arm and made her face him again.

"Before you start your campaign to boot me out," he said, "I think I have the right to know who you are and why you have the power to do it. I also thought I might thank you for saving my life."

Gypsy calmly removed her arm from his grasp. "It's enough that I know who *you* are, Mr. McCready. And don't feel you have to thank me for pulling you out of that plane. I did it for myself as much as I did it for you." With that, she turned on her heel and strode away.

Two hours later Gypsy was ready to leave Oshkosh. With the help of her father-in-law, Neal Gallagher, she finished storing her supplies in the front compartment of her own biplane. A canary-yellow 1928 Gipsy Moth, the craft was her namesake, and, these days, her only kindred spirit.

"I still can't figure why you changed your mind about competin' at Fond du Lac so all of a sudden," Neal remarked as he straightened with a grunt. "You won last year, after all."

Gypsy smiled. "Maybe I don't want to push my luck."

"Luck, my foot," he scoffed. "You're a damned good flier, Gypsy-girl, and you'd best be knowin' it."

Gypsy leaned against the fuselage of the Moth and folded her arms. "I'm feeling claustrophobic, Neal. I need to get out into the open air again. The convention's been fun, but eight days is enough. It's time to move on."

If she'd hoped to fool Neal, it didn't work. "It was the accident this afternoon that decided you, wasn't it?" he asked. "That's the true reason you're runnin' off."

"The accident has nothing to do with it," she snapped. When she saw the speculative look in his eyes, and the sadness, she softened. "All right, maybe it does. When that plane came down I saw Lon's accident all over again, like it was repeating itself. I guess it shook me up more than I thought it could."

After a pause Neal shook his head. "I feared as much." He came over to her and put his large hands on her shoulders. "Lon is gone. It does you no good to be dredgin' up old ghosts. Granted, the accidents were similar, but that's as far as it goes. Understand me?"

Gypsy nodded as she accepted her father-in-law's comfort. He was a huge, friendly Irishman with deep blue eyes set in a craggy, no-nonsense face, and she loved him for his concern. Lon had been his son. They'd shared their grief five years ago, and he alone knew what she was going through now.

Since Lon's death Gypsy had joined Neal at Gallagher Aviation down in Milwaukee as a flight instructor. She loved the work, but as her own father had put it years ago, the O'Haras were "born to the wanderlust," and she'd inherited a love of the open sky. Selling rides in a midwestern corn field seemed to be a habit she couldn't break. Every year from late July to the end of September she became a free agent, and that freedom was as close as she'd ever come to contentment.

She felt more than a twinge of guilt over leaving

Neal this time, though. Gallagher Aviation was in serious financial trouble due to the theft of two underinsured planes. She'd offered to stay, but he insisted she do what she had to do.

"By the way," he was saying, "did you talk to the EAA about that McCready fella?"

"I did." Gypsy's anger toward the journalist rekindled. She busied her hands tying a white silk scarf around her neck. "They told me he's leaving for New York today, and they don't want to risk offending the magazine he writes for. They're afraid the convention might get bad press." She stuffed her chin-length deep auburn hair beneath a leather helmet. Gone was the loose-fitting flight suit. In its place were tan trousers, a brown leather jacket, and calf-length boots. The scarf and the helmet completed the look of an old-time aviatrix. "If it were up to me, I'd have him brought up on charges and publicly flogged."

"Hmmph," came Neal's response. "What do you expect of a Scot, anyhow? Crazy, the lot o' them."

"Are you going straight back to Milwaukee?" Gypsy asked as she prepared to climb into the rear cockpit.

He frowned. "I have to. What with the money we lost from those planes, I don't know how much longer we'll stay in business. If I could only get me hands on that crackpot of an accountant..."

"We'll never see him again. I'll lay odds he left the state the day after the planes were stolen. Neal, if you'd like me to stay this summer, just say so. It doesn't feel right to me, leaving you with all this." Gypsy hesitated, giving him one last chance to change his mind.

"No, no." He waved her on. "Business has fallen off so much you'd have nothin' to do anyhow. This has all but ruined our reputation." When she opened her mouth to protest again he would have none of it. "Off with you, now. Go and do your barnstormin'. But keep in touch, girl."

He took her in his arms for a tight bear hug and Gypsy kissed him on the cheek. "I'll miss you. I'll drop you a card when I hit Hancock." When Neal released her she climbed up into the Moth and adjusted her goggles. As soon as she was ready she gave him a thumbs-up, and he nodded, pulling the propeller of the plane around ever so slowly. The impulse spring snapped, the rebuilt engine fired, and her beloved companion came to life once more.

Within a few minutes she was in the air, leaving Oshkosh behind, hoping to replace one set of memories with another. Anticipation lightened her mind. The next two months were hers to do as she chose. Somehow it seemed best to remember Lon by doing the thing they both loved most. She felt closer to him that way. She knew her annual barnstorming jaunts had become a kind of pilgrimage, a means to connect with the past and find that part of herself she'd lost.

Sometimes it worked. Sometimes it didn't.

Banking gently to the left, she headed for Hancock, her first stop.

"Hancock," Keane McCready muttered as he stopped his rented Volkswagen Rabbit in the center of the dirt road to consult his map. "Where the hell is Hancock?" What he discovered did nothing to brighten his mood. He'd missed the turnoff two miles back.

Damn Paul Daniels for sending him on this wild-goose chase! Keane's plans to return home to New York the previous day had been dashed the moment he called Daniels, his editor at *World View*. Still shaken from the accident, and angry at the woman he'd later found to be Gypsy Gallagher, he'd recounted their heated exchange to his boss. Immediately Daniels's interest kindled, no doubt prompted by the magazine's new publishing magnate, T. C. Bitteman. It had been Bitteman's idea to send Keane to Oshkosh in the first place, and now it seemed he had more surprises up his sleeve. The man wanted to widen *World View*'s focus, as if that were possible, with the addition of lighter, more entertaining articles. The world, Bitteman said, was "a dark, politically complicated place," and it was up to them, as a leading news publication, to brighten it with a bit of color. Oshkosh was a departure for them, but one he had high hopes for. Keane had been given the job.

Trouble had a way of following Keane from assignment to assignment, and his last one in Miami had proved no exception. Two prominent New York politicians had been involved in a drug scam, and Keane's subsequent story in *World View* had exposed them. Since then he'd received threats via organized crime, and both Bitteman and Daniels felt he should lie low for a while, at least until the two were formally indicted. What better place than the remote beauty of Wisconsin?

"Dammit, Paul, he's trying to punish me, isn't he?" Keane had railed when Bitteman's newest brainstorm was suggested—that he track down Gypsy Gallagher and use her as the focus of his article. Human interest, and all that.

"Is it my fault you opened your big mouth at the last staff meeting and told him he was turning *World View* into an adjunct of *People* magazine?" Daniels countered.

"I was right, and this proves it."

"You were also out of line. If it happens again you might find yourself writing only this kind of fluff. Come on, Keane. Wrap this story up, and you'll be off the hit list, I guarantee it. Besides, the boys from Miami still want to draft you into their ranks the hard way, so you *need* more time away. Think of it as a vacation and be thankful you're not in my shoes, stuck in an office with that blimp Bitteman breathing down my neck. He probably has my phone tapped . . ."

"I'm gonna get you for this, Paul," Keane had promised. "Some day, some way, when you least suspect it."

"I'll be quaking with fear. Just find your modern-day Amelia Earhart and make like a reporter."

And that was how he came to be lost somewhere in the back roads of rural Wisconsin, searching for a small farm community called Hancock and an auburn-haired spitfire in an antique biplane. When he'd asked after her the previous afternoon he'd been told she was already en route to Hancock from Oshkosh. If he wanted a story he'd have to follow her there. Stinson, his photographer, had commitments back in New York, so Keane had ventured on alone, carrying his own camera and feeling ridiculous.

Damn! He was an investigative reporter, not a personality chaser; he didn't belong here. He functioned best in trouble spots. He supposed it was his nature. It was also his nature to be curious, most times to a fault. From what he'd gathered, Gypsy Gallagher *was* an interesting woman, albeit a caustic one, and if the circumstances were different he might find her a challenging interview. For a moment he remembered her lightly freckled skin and those fiery emerald-green eyes, and smiled.

When he found the right road at last he told himself to look on the bright side. Even the worst-case scenario wasn't that bleak. The most she might do would be to force him up in her biplane only to push him out over the nearest lake. Sure, and if he survived that, he'd probably be fired for dereliction of duty.

Miami was looking better and better.

Gypsy circled low over the little farmhouse on the outskirts of Hancock, dipping one wing in greeting to several people who stood outside it. Her passenger was the thirteen-year-old girl who lived there, and Gypsy was giving her a bird's-eye view of her home that the girl would probably never forget.

It was late afternoon and she'd been hopping rides for two dollars a head since early morning. The sun had begun to sink lower on the horizon and the balmy air of late summer sang through the flying wires of the Moth. With the gentlest of touches she eased it down to earth once more, back to the green grassy field she'd gotten permission from the owner to use. A few cars remained, people who wanted to fly next or who simply wanted to watch.

When the Moth rolled to a stop they rushed over to congratulate the girl on her first time in the air and ask her how it felt. A great majority of them had never flown, and Gypsy loved to see their faces come to life when they spotted a familiar place on the ground. The exhilaration she experienced viewing it all through their eyes never faded.

"Did you see, Daddy, did you see?" the girl called as Gypsy helped her down from the forward cockpit. "I loved it!"

Her father, a tall work-worn man, gestured toward their truck. "Time to be gettin' home. Fun's over."

"Can we come back tomorrow?" she asked him, her face flushed and her long blond hair in disarray. "I want to talk to Gypsy about learning to be a pilot. Oh, Daddy, please?"

The man glanced at Gypsy, his expression sober. "You been puttin' ideas in my girl's head?" Before Gypsy had a chance to tell him otherwise, he went on. "You can live your life however you see fit, but that don't mean you can plant ideas about it in somebody else. Come on, Karen, we're leavin'."

"But Daddy, she wasn't—"

Gypsy stepped forward and rested a hand on the girl's shoulder. "I would never try to influence your daughter, sir. I'm sure she has a mind of her own, and when the time is right, she'll use it. For now, if I've helped broaden her horizons a little, I'm satisfied." Her voice softened. "I loved having you along for a ride, Karen, and the next time I come through you're welcome to fly with me again, okay?"

"Okay. I guess I have to help Mom tomorrow, anyway. Just don't forget to come back."

"I promise I won't forget." Gypsy smiled, then turned her over to her father. "She's all yours."

He merely grunted and led his daughter away to their truck.

Gypsy removed her helmet and shook out her hair. She encountered this kind of attitude often. It was a sticky situation to become an idol to a child and a threat to a parent. She hoped she'd gotten herself, and Karen, off the hook gracefully.

"That's it for today, folks," she told the small crowd that surrounded the plane. "I'll be here tomorrow, and if the weather's anything like today, it'll be terrific for flying."

"I just might take you up on that," a deep male voice said from the sidelines.

Gypsy looked up to find Keane McCready making his way toward her, a sight so unexpected her mouth dropped open. "You! What on earth are you *doing* here?"

"Thought you could get rid of me that easily, huh?" He smiled and waved to the last of the people as they left the field. "I thought you might like to know that Dick Russell is doing okay. He's got a broken ankle, is all. I wasn't sure if you stuck around long enough to find out yesterday."

"I found out." Gypsy was determined not to let his sarcasm get to her. Though she'd recognized him instantly, he looked different than he had after the accident. He wore neat, if wrinkled, dark brown slacks and a soft cream-colored shirt. His hair was combed and his face clean, revealing high cheekbones and a square, resolute jaw. He looked like a man who was accustomed to getting what he wanted, by whatever means possible. And she had a sinking feeling that he wanted something from her.

"Is that all you came here to tell me?" she asked. "Or did your first experience in a biplane bring you clamoring for more?"

He glanced away for a moment, then cleared his throat. "To tell you the truth, I never want to go up in one of those things again. The only reason I did it in the first place was because I felt I needed to know what the sensation was like in order to write about it."

"You could have done that in an ordinary way, with an ordinary pilot."

He shook his head. "No, I couldn't. I was assigned to write about the spirit of Oshkosh, and the aerobatics display is a large part of that."

"Maybe." Gypsy studied him as she removed her gloves. "You still haven't answered my question, McCready. Why did you follow me here?"

"Now that's kind of a long story." He began to fidget under her steady gaze.

"Make it as short as humanly possible, please, and then go. I have things to do." Gypsy wondered at her reaction to him. She'd never considered herself a rude person, but this man had brought out the worst in her from the moment they met. She thought she detected an answering spark in his blue eyes as he adjusted his stance and faced her directly.

"Do you have any idea," he said, voice low and intense, "what I have gone through to find you? When I learned you left Oshkosh I had a devil of a time getting anyone to tell me where you were headed. You'll be happy to know your fellow pilots are very protective of you. When I explained that I only wanted to interview you they finally told me you were on your way to Hancock. 'Where in Hancock?' I asked. 'The nearest empty field,' they informed me. 'Okay,' said I. 'Why not?' So I rented a car, got lost twice on back roads, drove all day without a meal so I wouldn't miss you, and what do I get for my troubles? 'Make it short and then go.' Lady, that is one hell of a welcome."

Gypsy had stopped listening to his diatribe when she heard the word *interview*. "What do you mean, interview me?" she asked quietly when he finished.

"I called my editor the day of the accident," he explained. "I told him you saved my life, our publisher liked the angle, and the next thing I knew you were my new assignment. They want me out of the way for a while, anyway, so this whole thing must've seemed like kismet." He held up a hand when Gypsy started to speak. "No, wait till I'm finished. I told them you already hated me on sight, but it didn't seem to make any difference. They refused to take no for an answer. So here I am, tired, hungry, and put out. What do you say we get it over with tonight, and then in the morning I'd be happy to leave you to your sharecropping, or whatever you call it. I'll tell Daniels I did the best I could."

"Barnstorming," she corrected flatly.

"Right, barnstorming. Now—"

"No."

He stopped short and stared. "What?"

Gypsy stepped forward, hands on her hips. "I said, no. No interview. Now, if you want to stay in Hancock for the night, by all means stay. Get yourself a bite to eat and rest up for another long drive. But first leave my field, and leave me. There must be plenty of women pilots you can talk to who are more interesting."

"Oh, at least a hundred," he drawled. "But I'm afraid you're it. I may not like the idea myself, but when I have a job to do, I do it. I just need to know how you started on the air-show circuit, a little about your background, and your future plans."

"You said your magazine wanted you out of the way for a while," Gypsy ventured, as determined as ever to get rid of him, but curious nonetheless.

McCready sighed and began to lean against the wing strut of the Moth.

"Don't do that!"

He straightened swiftly and folded his arms across his chest. "Sorry," he said, eyebrows lifting. "I'm an investigative reporter, Ms. Gallagher, and I usually do political and criminal pieces. As a result of my last article I have some very influential people . . . upset with me."

"So you were sent here as punishment, is that it?"

"No, that's not it! I'm just lying low for a while, until this thing blows over and I can go back."

"And you actually abhor the idea of interviewing me in the meantime?" Gypsy asked with a slight smile. The sun behind McCready had created an incongruous halo around his head, and she found the image absurdly amusing.

He thought for a second before he answered her. "At the beginning, yes, I guess I did. But the more I talk to you, the more of a challenge you become. I think I might stick around out of sheer perversity just to see what you have to offer."

He looked her up and down with a provocative

grin and Gypsy felt a sudden thrill of energy that startled her. She shook her head in confusion. "Why me? What did I do to deserve this honor? I'm curious."

"You certainly are. Seriously, though—you saved my life back at Oshkosh. I never would have gotten away from that plane in time if you hadn't pushed me, and you risked your own life to do that. Now to me, that's pretty interesting. Also, from what I could gather, you're a damn good pilot, and flying around the Midwest selling rides is not my idea of a normal occupation for a woman, pilot or no. You're what we call a 'personality,' and as such, my editor thinks you'd make a fascinating story. So, how about it?"

"No." Gypsy turned to rummage in the Moth's storage compartment for her cooking supplies.

"Why not?" he persisted.

She set the supply sack on the ground by the plane and turned back to him, pushing a lock of hair from her eyes. "I'm not obligated to give you a reason, McCready. I'm not obligated to give you anything. So if you'd excuse me, I'd like to fix my dinner now."

He stood quietly for a time, watching her as she fished about in the sack for cooking utensils. Then he nodded to himself. "Okay, I suppose I can play it your way. I'm going back to my car, and I'm going to wait for you to finish dinner." He glanced with envy at an unopened can of beef stew and shrugged. "By then you may be so sick of my company you'll talk my ear off just to get rid of me."

"You can stay there till hell freezes over," Gypsy murmured as she concentrated on her tasks. Out of the corner of her eye she saw him withdraw and walk slowly toward his car. Would he really stay and wait her out? She still found it hard to believe he'd come all this way in search of her. She was well known enough on the circuit and had been approached several times by various flying magazines for interviews, but never one of *World View*'s magnitude. She had no desire to expose herself in a publication of that sort. Some things were better left unsaid. Besides, she sensed McCready was holding something back about his own reasons for being here.

Sighing, she lit the charcoal briquettes in her little tin stove, opened the can of stew with a metal can opener, and placed it over the heat. Then she stretched out on the grass and leaned back against the Moth's left wheel to watch the sunset while the stew warmed. When it came to patience, she could outlast a hyperactive journalist any day. The moment the sun went down he'd scurry for cover in some nice, comfy motel.

Her eyes flicked to her right of their own volition. Even over the distance that separated them she could see McCready was smiling.

CHAPTER
Two

KEANE'S STOMACH STARTED TO rumble about
thirty minutes into his vigil. He leaned across the
seat and poked around in the glove compartment
for a half-eaten candy bar he'd stashed there that
morning.

"The least she could do is invite me over for
some food," he grumbled as he peeled the wrapper
from the gooey chocolate.

How long was she planning to keep this game
up? He fully intended to stay put until she softened,
and his resolve surprised him. Sure, he didn't want
to risk losing his job, or anything else of vital im-
portance, should the Miami Mob Squad get their
hands on him. But it wasn't just that. He'd been
threatened before, and by worse. Could it be that
lovely Gypsy Gallagher *had* become a challenge to
him? And if so, did he feel that challenge as a journalist, or as a man? As a journalist he had to admit
there might be a potential story in her. Not a great
one, maybe, but a good one. And as a man—he'd
have to reserve judgment on that. There was more
going on behind those emerald eyes, he suspected,
than he or anyone else knew.

* * *

Gypsy fidgeted.

She'd long ago given up on the stew. It was impossible to sit there and eat when she could feel McCready's eyes on her every move. Now and then she risked a surreptitious glance in his direction, and each time it was the same. He'd be sitting sideways in the driver's seat of his car, elbows on his knees, either watching her or gazing at nothing in particular. When he began to munch on the candy she suppressed a faint twinge of guilt. If no one ate the stew she'd have to throw it out.

Stop it, she told herself. He can go into town if he's hungry. After all, the man wants to invade your privacy, tell your secrets to the world to make a buck. Again she wondered—why?

The sun, now low on the horizon, cast a warm orange glow over the field. A slight breeze began to blow and Gypsy lifted her face to it, letting it waft through her hair. She closed her eyes. Maybe when she opened them he would be gone.

What a picture she makes! Keane marveled as the woman across from him raised her head and stretched one long, jeans-clad leg out in front of her. Silhouetted in profile against a burnt-orange sky, she looked like a female Red Baron, complete with flowing scarf and leather jacket. So solitary, yet so content in her aloneness.

Quietly he retrieved his Nikon from the back seat, careful not to disturb her so she wouldn't move. He clicked off five shots in quick succession.

At the sound her head whipped around and she looked him square in the eye, mumbling something he couldn't make out. It was probably just as well.

Keane shrugged and smiled, then clicked off one more as she turned her back on him with exaggerated indifference. She had spirit, he'd give her that. He wondered if she planned to spend the night beside her plane, all alone in a dark and empty field. The thought made him uneasily protective, and he shook himself.

A renewed rumble in his stomach put a stop to his wayward mind. Damn, he was starved, not to mention thirsty. Maybe he should go into town for a little while, then come back. The idea was appealing, but after waging a small war with his body he figured he could take it for a couple more hours. What if he left, only to return and find her gone? He'd never be able to track her down a second time.

He leaned his head on the doorframe and waited. Surely she'd take pity on him soon.

Gypsy stood and walked toward the tail of the Moth, her back still to McCready. She was angry as hell at him for taking those photographs without her permission. But then, he couldn't use them if he didn't have a story to accompany them, could he? Dammit, why didn't he say something? The silence became more deafening each second this stupid battle of wills went on. When it got dark it would be time to roll out her sleeping bag, and she certainly didn't want him around when she settled in for the night.

So much for peace. Her thoughts spiraled back to another summer night five years ago. Tired from a day of hopping rides, she and Lon had stretched out beneath the wing of his Travel Air and made love in a field of green-gold hay. It had been so special, the love they shared. Their marriage was the single most important thing in her life—

Gypsy shook her head and rested it against the bright yellow tail of the Moth. Its smooth surface felt cool next to her cheek. She had to get rid of Keane McCready somehow. He was bringing too many memories back to life.

She turned to face him, but made no effort to bridge the distance between them. He would have to enter her territory, on her terms. "McCready!" she called. "I have some leftover stew. You're welcome to it if you're hungry." Funny, it didn't come out sounding half as antagonistic as she'd intended.

"So," McCready said as he finished the last of the stew, "exactly what kind of airplane is this?"

Gypsy sat, arms crossed over her chest, studying him. Darkness had fallen so she'd lit a portable lantern and placed it between them. The air was growing chill and she was thankful for her insulated leather jacket. McCready had only his suit coat. "I thought we agreed," she reminded him. "No interview. Food in exchange for consideration."

He laughed. "Don't *I* have the right to a little curiosity? It's a simple enough question, off the record."

He continued to smile at her and again Gypsy felt that queer little thrill rush through her. It was hard not to notice the dimple in his right cheek and the way the lantern light played off the golden strands in his hair. Up close this way she could smell the faint musk scent of his cologne. How long had it been since she'd noticed those things about a man, or been so uncomfortably aware of them? She forced her mind back to his question. "It's a 1928 deHavilland Gipsy Moth. G-I-P-S-Y. It's a type of engine."

He nodded, and she could see the wheels turning in his mind. "It seems to be in excellent condition," he remarked, touching the underside of one bottom wing.

"I bought it a few years back and restored it. The only modification I made was to add a new radio."

"I'm impressed. I've never met a woman as... mechanically inclined as you." He paused. "As a matter of fact, I've never met a woman even remotely like you."

His eyes were intent on her face, and Gypsy sensed a sudden, new tension between them. Was he aware of the feelings he brought out in her? How could he be? She'd only just become aware of them herself.

When she remained silent for more than a few seconds McCready shook his head in frustration. "Most times I'm very good at either putting people at ease or pressuring them into spilling their foulest secrets. Believe it or not, I'm trying to put you at ease."

Gypsy lifted her chin a fraction. "I'll be at ease as soon as you leave me alone," she said. "I invited you over here so you wouldn't starve yourself to death, but now that you've eaten you have no reason to stay."

He laughed again, this time bitterly. "What did I ever do to you, Gypsy Gallagher? Did you resent saving my life so much that you feel you have to punish me for it?"

"I helped you because you were a human being. I did not resent it and I have nothing against you. I just want to be left alone." She stood and grabbed the lantern, using its light to find her sleeping bag.

McCready decided retreat was better than attack and changed the subject. "Isn't it a little dangerous, spending the night alone way out here?"

Gypsy shrugged as she spread the bag out on the grass beneath the wing. "It's safer than being locked indoors in the city," she replied. "Now, if you'll excuse me, I'm very tired. It's been a long day and I have to go into town for gas first thing in the morning."

She heard nothing behind her for a time and she thought maybe he'd gone. Then he shuffled his feet and said, "All right, all right. I'll leave. But I want to give you a few things to think about first. I did a little checking before I followed you here and I found you're part owner of a general aviation facility in Milwaukee. Gallagher Aviation."

Gypsy turned, startled but not terribly surprised that he knew. It wouldn't do to underestimate the man. "And?" she asked.

"And," he continued, "I know there's been some financial difficulty lately. Something about a couple of stolen planes that were underinsured."

She allowed herself a slight smile. "You're good, McCready. You've only known me for two days and already you've discovered one of my 'foul secrets.' I don't see what it has to do with you, though."

He shifted his weight from one foot to the other, his form barely visible in the diffused light from the small lantern. "Since you refused even to consider the idea from the start, we never got around to discussing what this interview might be worth to you. How positive exposure in a national magazine would help generate more business than Gallagher Aviation could handle. By answering a few questions you could literally turn your life around—and your partner's. Like I said, think about it. I'll be back in the morning."

Anger built inside Gypsy as he turned to go. How dare he try to use Gallagher Aviation to blackmail her into agreeing to his precious interview! As he neared his car she found her voice. "McCready!"

He stopped, his back to her.

"Tell your editor he can go to hell."

He chuckled in the darkness. "I have, many times. It doesn't do any good."

A sharp, pungent smell woke her early the next morning. Turning over in her bag, Gypsy opened her eyes a fraction and focused on a pair of impeccable leather street shoes. She raised her head when they shifted, then wished she hadn't. "Oh, no. McCready!"

"One and the same." He stood, all smiles, his arms folded. Several cans of gasoline rested on the grass beside him. "I wasn't sure how much this crate took, so I estimated high. Is regular all right?"

Gypsy struggled to a sitting position and pushed her hair away from one eye. "I should have known you'd be back," she sighed.

"I'm a man of my word, but I never let integrity get the better of me."

"Don't make it sound so admirable." She stood and rolled up her bag, stowing it in the plane. Coffee. She needed coffee before she could even begin to deal with him. When he opened his mouth to speak again she held up a hand. "Not yet. Let me make some coffee first, okay? Oh, and by the way —don't ever call the Moth a crate."

His golden-brown eyebrows lifted. "Grouchy in the morning, aren't we? That's all right, I'm getting used to waiting when it comes to you."

He sat cross-legged on the ground and watched her as she measured instant coffee into a plastic cup. She paused and made herself ask, "Would you like some?"

"No, thanks, I had breakfast in town. Kind of you to offer, though."

She nodded and poured some bottled water into a pan, then set it on the tin stove. She felt his eyes on her as she prepared to light the coals. "You'd better make sure those gasoline fumes are blowing away from us," she remarked nonchalantly, then smiled as he leaped up and moved the cans a safe distance from them.

"I called my editor last night," he told her when he sat down again. "I explained to him that you were less than enthusiastic about this project."

"Oh?" Gypsy asked warily, combing her fingers through her hair in a vain effort to tame its sometimes unruly curl. "And what was his reply?"

"Aside from a few graphic anatomical references concerning yours truly, he wondered why a journalist who's gotten presidents and kings to talk to him can't convince a modern-day Amelia Earhart to give him the time of day. Then he got mad."

Gypsy raised her eyes heavenward. "Sometimes you sound like a broken record, you know that? Is there anything you care about other than your all-important interview?"

"As a matter of fact, there is," he said after a quiet moment. "I have an eight-year-old son who's been waiting three months for me to pick him up and take him to my place for a visit." He frowned, and the dimple in his cheek all but vanished. "The problem is, I'm never home for any decent length of time. If it's not Washington or Miami, it's some godforsaken field in Wisconsin."

A new current of emotion underscored his words and Gypsy looked up from her coffee. "Are you trying to blame that on me? Besides, I got the impression you loved your work. That would include the traveling too, wouldn't it?"

He nodded. "Yes, it includes the traveling, as long as there's something for me to do when I reach wherever it is I'm going. Thus far, all I've done here is waste my time trying to cajole a hardheaded female flying ace into giving me a few hours of her time in exchange for the best publicity she'll ever get. Dammit, woman, anyone else in your position would jump at the opportunity. What in hell are you afraid of?"

I'm afraid you'll find out too much, she wanted to shout. Instead she said, "I detect desperation in your voice."

He eyed her, cupping his hands beneath his chin. "If it's desperation that'll change your mind, yes I'm desperate. Haven't you got it through your head yet that I want to go home? I've had my fill of wide-open spaces. I crave the clutter of the city. Like the song says, I belong to it."

"Is that the whole reason?"

"It'll have to do."

"And you have no real desire to find out about me?"

"None whatever." He let his gaze sweep over her from boot to head. "Aside from the fact that I find you to be an incredibly attractive woman, and be-hind your veneer a frightened one, you're about as interesting to me as the Shah of Iran."

"That's not what you said last night."

"So I'm fickle." He shrugged.

"What a comfort." Finishing her coffee, Gypsy stood and stretched, then grabbed several items from the Moth. When she turned she surprised her-self by saying, "Do me a favor, and I promise you I'll think about this."

McCready's shoulders straightened. "What favor?"

"I was going to buy a few supplies when I went into town for gas this morning. If I gave you a list, could you go and get them for me? It's late, and people are going to be here soon. You have a car and I want to take a bath."

"Sounds promising. The fact that you're willing to think about it, and the bath."

Gypsy shot him a reproving glance. "Will you do it?"

"Give me your list and I'm gone. And forgive my denseness, but where can you take a bath around here?"

She pointed. "Behind that copse of trees at the edge of the field there's a small pond. I saw it when I flew over."

"What do you do when there isn't a handy pond?" he asked.

"I haven't agreed to an interview yet, so save your questions," she warned him. "Here's the list and some money; don't hurry back."

He tipped an imaginary hat. "Yes, ma'am. You want me to circle around the block a few times when I get back so I don't catch you au naturel in yonder pond?"

Gypsy was already walking away. "Don't push your luck, Mr. Wordsmith," she called over her shoulder. "How do you know I'm not conning you into leaving while I pack up and fly to Iowa?"

"Because even though I've only known you for two days, I know when you're lying. Reporter's instinct. I think it's got to do with body language."

Gypsy luxuriated in the feel of the cool water on her skin. The pond was perfect, secluded and peaceful. Birds sang in the trees overhead and sunlight slanted through the branches, turning the morning air to a golden mist. She'd left her clothes on a low bank next to a pile of clean ones. Hopefully McCready would dawdle in Hancock so she could make the most of her privacy.

Her thoughts returned to his proposed interview, and the incentive he'd given her. She doubted he knew just how much trouble Gallagher Aviation was in. It might take more than a little publicity to bring them the amount of business they'd need to get out of the red. But then, *World View* wasn't a "little" magazine, and the business it could generate was more than they had now. What better solution could they find at this point?

She knew Neal had thought about selling, though he'd never actually mentioned it. She suspected he was glad she'd be out of the way for the summer so he wouldn't have to go on hiding the worry in his eyes. If Gallagher Aviation failed, Gypsy would have no trouble finding a job as a flight instructor for another facility. Neal, on the other hand, had nothing else. The business he and Gypsy's father had built back in the early sixties meant the world to him. He was too old to fly and too proud to acknowledge it, something she knew cut him to the bone.

McCready had offered her a way to ease the burden on her father-in-law, if even for a short time. How could she turn it down and go back to face Neal at summer's end? Yet how could she guarantee that the journalist wouldn't dig too deeply into her past?

Gypsy dunked her head and began to wash her hair with a cake of mild soap. Out of frustration she rubbed more in than she needed to and ended up with lather running down her face. She squeezed her eyes shut and persevered until she was sure the dirt and grime were removed. Open cockpits would never be conducive to shining, dust-free hair, helmet or no.

A noise off to her right caused her to slow her vigorous scrubbing. As she waited for it to repeat itself the air chilled her exposed skin and she shivered. It was just a rabbit coming for a drink, she reasoned. But then a twig snapped and a definite sound of footsteps echoed in the enclosed area. A rabbit hopped; it didn't stride with the purposeful gait of a man!

Whoever it was barely got out the word, "Hey..." before she launched the cake of soap like a missile toward the voice. A second later she heard a sharp *"Ow!"* and the sound of someone falling rear first onto the grassy bank.

Of course. Who else could it be but McCready? Gypsy dunked again and swished her head around to remove the suds. Damn the man! He'd most likely gotten a good look at her, naked from the waist up, her head and face covered with a mound of white foam. Wonderful.

When she surfaced she kept only her head above water. McCready sat on the bank, a hand to one eye, moaning. It front of him were her clothes, the old ones and the clean ones, both bundles floating on top of the pond where his foot must have knocked them.

Gypsy tried to retrieve them before they sank but she couldn't manage it without coming halfway out of the water, and that she wasn't prepared to do. So she watched, stymied, as the bundles first submerged, then came up a moment later, soaked. "You imbecile!" she cried. "What the hell do you think you're doing walking in on me like this? Look at my clothes!"

McCready made a halfhearted effort to stand, then decided against it and sank back to the bank. Still holding his hand to his left eye, he peered at her through the other. "What the hell are you doing throwing two-ton cakes of soap at people's eyes?" he countered, as angry as she.

"I didn't know you from Jack the Ripper. I couldn't see."

He smirked. "Jack the Ripper on a farm? You're the one who's lethal, lady, not me. I only came back to tell you my car won't start."

"You could have told me that from the other side of the trees, or you could have waited." She tried to look as dignified as possible as she stood in the now-cold pond. It wasn't easy. "I suppose you got an eyeful," she mumbled.

"An eye full of soap is what I got. I didn't have a chance to see anything else—and at this point I don't even regret it." He leaned forward, grabbed the sleeve of her floating blouse, and held it to his eye, ignoring her.

Gypsy fumed. In a low, deadly voice she asked, "Would you please leave so I can get out of here and put on my *wet, muddy* clothes?"

He glanced at the blouse he held and had the grace to look mildly sheepish. "If I turn my back can I trust you?"

She tried for a laugh, but it came out more like a cross between a sneeze and a sob. "The only thing you can trust me to do is take you up in the Moth and dump you out over a cow pasture—if I don't catch pneumonia first."

He nodded and winced. "Somehow I knew you'd say something like that. I'll wait by the car if I can make it that far." He pulled himself to his feet and for the first time faced Gypsy directly.

She realized, belatedly, that she'd risen partway out of the water and her breasts were again exposed. Quickly she went back down, but not before her eyes had met his. The intensity of his stare touched a chord deep inside her body and she held her breath until the sensation of weightlessness passed.

Neither of them spoke for several seconds, then McCready took an awkward step back and cleared his throat. "I, uh . . . uhh . . . oh, God." Leaving her clothes to soak, he staggered quickly off beyond the trees.

Gypsy waited a full thirty seconds, expecting him to reappear the instant she left the pond. When she detected no further movement she gathered her clothes and spent a frustrating few minutes trying to pull them over her body. She'd have to get some fresh ones from the Moth and come back here to change again. So much for tranquil interludes. So much for privacy and the freedom to be alone. So much for peace of mind.

She squared her shoulders and trudged to the plane, her socks squishing in her boots.

McCready was hunched over the engine of his car when she got there, mumbling to himself. Gypsy sighed and postponed the change of clothes. "A white Rabbit, huh?" she asked as she came up behind him. "It doesn't seem your style."

"It's good on gas." His hands moved over the small engine, pulling here and tugging there, accomplishing nothing.

"So what's wrong with it?"

He hung his head. "If I knew that, I'd fix it, wouldn't I? Damn German engines." When Gypsy inadvertently dripped on him he straightened and moved to one side. "You're supposed to be the expert mechanic. Have a look."

"If you don't mind me flooding it," she quipped, brushing wet hair from her face. After a cursory inspection and some well-placed questions she pronounced, "I think it's the alternator. Unless you can get a transplant, I'm afraid your Rabbit is dead."

He smiled without humor. "Thank you, Doc Gallagher. Can I get one in town?"

Gypsy thought about that. She'd been to Hancock once before, and all it had was one small gas station/garage. His chances of finding a foreign part were almost nil. "Even if they could order it, it'd take a day or so," she told him. "And there's no car rental agency, either. Your best bet would be Libertyville, about sixty miles southwest of here."

McCready remained silent for a few moments before he asked, "And where are you heading when you finish in Hancock?"

"Libertyville," she blurted without thinking. When his expression changed from frustration to dawning pleasure, she knew what he had on his calculating little mind. She took an automatic step backward. "No, McCready..."

He chuckled, amused by her discomfort. "Come on, Gallagher, you owe me a favor. It's the least I deserve for getting socked in the eye with a bar of soap."

He advanced on her, and as he drew closer Gypsy saw that his left eye had begun to swell and turn a nasty shade of purple. She felt the edge of a wing against her shoulder blades and realized she'd let him back her up to the Moth. "Guilt won't work," she said, raising her chin. "If I flew you to Libertyville I'd have to have a damn good reason. You could always take a bus."

He lowered his head and the masculine scent of him filled her nostrils. His face was just inches from hers and she saw her own reflection in the clear sky blue of his eyes. "Okay," he murmured. "How's this for a good reason? If I take a bus you may never see me again and you'd lose your chance to save your business. On the other hand, if you flew me to Libertyville we could conduct the interview there, I could rent another car, and I'd be out of your hair for good. We'd be doing each other a favor, so no one comes out the loser. What do you say?"

His voice had lowered to a husky whisper and against her will Gypsy began to weaken. Don't be an idiot, she warned herself. This man could probably read a phone book out loud and make it sound like a come-on. Her own eyes traveled to his chest, exposed by a partially unbuttoned dark blue shirt, before she brought them back to his bruised face. "I must be out of my mind."

"Come on." He smiled. "My company can't be that bad."

She sidestepped him, then took a deep breath, folding her arms across her wet, clingy blouse. His gaze followed the movement. "I have one stipulation," she told him slowly.

"Name it."

"I control the direction your questions take. If you ask me something I don't care to answer, you'll get off the subject. Clear? My personal life is just that. Personal."

He studied her as he considered her words. "You know, of course, that by giving me the impression you have something to hide, you're only piquing my professional curiosity."

She looked away from him. "Be that as it may, those are my terms. Now, do you agree or not? Because I'd just as soon leave you here to fend for yourself."

McCready spread his arms and backed off.

"Okay, I guess I can live with that. You have your-self a deal. You really ought to go change, you know, before you catch a chill. I don't want my pilot getting sick on me. You might have a sneezing fit and run smack into the side of a hill."

Without a word Gypsy gathered some clothes from the plane and started again for the trees. He had agreed too easily. She should have known that her ultimatum would be the same as dangling meat in front of a shark.

"Hey!" he shouted behind her.

She turned and waited while he caught up.

"Let's make it official with a handshake, shall we? That's usually the way things are done."

She saw his hand coming toward her as though it were disembodied and floating in midair. Fasci-nated, she watched as her own reached out to meet it, then felt the warmth of his skin on hers. Again the thrill. "No way is this going to work, McCready," she murmured.

"We'll see about that. Stranger things have hap-pened." His hand lingered a few seconds longer than it had to before he turned and walked back to his car. He was whistling.

Gypsy shook her head and whispered a silent prayer.

CHAPTER
Three

"For two days in Hancock she had great weather," Keane grumbled, unable to hear his own voice because the wind snatched it away the moment he opened his mouth. "For me, it rains."

He was securely strapped into the front cockpit of the Moth, looking down on a blanket of gray clouds from six thousand feet up. They'd risen above the worst of the rain, but mist fogged his goggles and he was unable to see anything. Not that there was much to see.

Gypsy had seemed blithely unconcerned on take-off. "This is nothing," she assured him. "A sprinkle. It's supposed to taper off by noon."

It didn't feel like nothing to Keane. His stomach did flip-flops every time they hit some turbulence, and at times it seemed the little biplane would shake itself apart at the seams. His last experience in the air had left him a bit paranoid and he wished the thirty-minute trip was over and they were safe on the ground in Libertyville.

Gypsy had stored his photographic equipment and his suitcase in the compartment in front of his feet, and he wondered if the delicate camera would still be intact when they landed. Chin up, old boy, he told himself. You made your bed, now you have to lie in it. Though, since she only carried one sleeping bag with her, he wasn't at all sure how that might work out.

His car's failing alternator had been a convenient accident that tipped the scales in his favor. If he'd done it on purpose she would have seen right through him. As it was, she'd had no recourse but to take him along. For better or worse she'd agreed to the interview, and now it was up to him to follow through. Excepting this roller coaster ride, he found he actually looked forward to it. Fate was playing strange games with him of late.

He turned as best he could in the seat and craned his neck to look at her. At the moment she was indistinguishable from himself, what with her helmet, goggles, and that silk scarf flying out behind her. She reminded him of Snoopy in his beloved Sopwith Camel, and Keane smiled, if briefly, at the image. The Moth was no doghouse, but a precision instrument, and only her skill at the rudder kept them from meeting the ground the hard way.

She gave him a thumbs-up signal, no doubt to reassure him, and he returned it with a broad smile, determined not to seem a coward. Then the plane dipped, his stomach flopped, and they began their descent to the town of Libertyville.

The rain was indeed beginning to let up when they touched down at the municipal airfield to refuel. Keane pulled himself out of the plane to stretch his cramped legs and find something to drink.

Gypsy jumped down beside him, removing her helmet and shaking out her dark auburn hair. "If you need a bathroom break, take it now; otherwise it's back to the bushes." She peered at him, suspicious. "You're not sick to your stomach, are you? You look a little green around the mouth."

Keane drew himself up to his full height and found he was still more or less looking her straight in the eye. "I'm fine," he stated in an attempt to convince his wayward stomach as well as her. "I always turn green in damp weather. Family trait." He smiled, but it probably came off as a grimace.

"Right." She nodded. "I'm going into the office to find a map and check out the latest weather reports. Meet me back here in ten minutes."

"Ja wohl." He watched her walk away toward the small, L-shaped building with the control tower jutting up from one end. She had a fantastically sexy walk, he realized. Almost a mannish gait, though she couldn't stop her hips from swaying the tiniest little bit, which reaffirmed her femininity. Her legs, encased in those leather boots, were long and lithe; and despite the way she felt about him and the proposed article, he was unable to suppress a current of longing. You hang around her for any length of time, he warned himself, and you'd better hope one of those ponds is nearby. A very cold pond.

When she disappeared inside the office he shook his head and asked the man who gassed up the plane where the rest rooms were. Once inside, he understood why the jerk had stared at him. His eye was now black, with tinges of maroon on the edges. The swelling had gone down, but he still looked like a Golden Gloves reject. "He probably thinks I'm a battered husband," he murmured as he studied his reflection in the mirror.

He returned to the plane with renewed determination not to let Gypsy Gallagher run the show. This was his interview, and he intended to conduct it in any way he saw fit, her conditions be damned. She was obviously afraid he'd dig deeper than she liked. There must be a reason.

"My father and Neal Gallagher were childhood friends back in County Meath, Ireland. In 1935 they immigrated to the United States, recruited some veteran World War I pilots, and formed an air circus."

Gypsy leaned back against the Moth's fuselage and stared at the lantern which rested between her and Keane McCready. Except for that one container of light it was pitch black in the uncultivated potato field she'd chosen to fly out of. Crickets chirped in the nearby foliage, and the clouds overhead hid the moon and stars.

McCready sat attentive, a thick notepad resting on his knees and a pencil in his hand, taking down her words in an odd kind of personal shorthand. She hadn't let him use his portable tape recorder for fear it would catch too much, and to her surprise he hadn't argued. He had turned from an obnoxious busybody to a complete professional, phrasing his questions in such a way that it seemed she volunteered the information instead of merely responding. She began to relax. This might not be so bad after all.

"What exactly is an air circus?" he asked now, the tip of his pencil poised on his upper lip.

"It's an air show that travels from town to town. The pilots do stunt flying, sell rides, provide refreshments. Neal and my father managed to scrape enough money together to buy two biplanes in good condition. They painted them bright green and yellow and billed themselves as 'O'Hara and Gallagher, the Flying Irishmen.'" She smiled, wistful. "Those must have been the days. Fliers were either heroes or just plain crazy, depending on which way you looked at it. The fascination was strong. It was the time of Lucky Lindy and Amelia Earhart, Wiley Post . . ."

"How long were they with the flying circus?" McCready asked, nudging her thoughts back on track.

"About six years, until World War II. They enlisted and when it was all over they'd lost touch with one another. Eventually they married and had one child each. With new families to support neither one of them ever went back to stunt flying."

"And your mother? Tell me about her."

Gypsy frowned. "I barely remember her. She died of pneumonia when I was very young and Papa raised me on his own. He never remarried. He was a good man." She didn't realize she'd trailed off until a couple of minutes later she snapped back with a start.

McCready watched her intently.

"What are you staring at?" she asked, suddenly irritated.

"You," he replied. "This is the first time I've had the privilege to observe you when you haven't been angry about something. I'm savoring the moment."

"You're also making me angry again." She wondered what it was about the man that brought out these strong emotional reactions in her. The warm diffused light softened the planes and angles of his face, but his eyes never lost that sparkle of mischief, of deviltry. His professional demeanor was designed to put her at ease, while underneath his impish counterpart was grinning, just waiting for her to slip up.

"Sorry." He smiled. "We wouldn't want that, would we?"

Gypsy nodded in agreement. "You wouldn't want to make me really angry. That's when I'll start advertising you as a wing walker."

His smile weakened a fraction. "I'll keep that in mind."

"Good. I think you've gotten enough out of me tonight, and I for one am bushed." She stood and pulled her sleeping bag from the Moth.

McCready sat quietly as she unrolled it, then cleared his throat. "At the risk of offending you yet again . . . where am I supposed to sleep?"

She'd been waiting for him to mention that. With a flourish, she indicated the plane's two open cockpits. "You have your choice of the forward or rear cabin. I suppose I *could* spare a blanket."

He sighed and nodded. "I made my own bed, now I have to lie in it, is that the idea?"

"That's the idea."

After a long, speculative pause, he stood and gathered his notes. "A wing walker, huh?"

"Just like in the old days." Gypsy smiled. "No safety harness, no nothing except your own two feet."

He looked once at the Moth's bottom wing, once at the black sky, and once at the few lights of Libertyville off in the distance beyond the field. "Where's the blanket?"

* * *

"This'll only take a couple of minutes. You're not in any hurry to get back, are you?" McCready asked, fishing in his pockets for change for the pay phone inside Libertyville's one drug store.

Gypsy glanced out at the overcast sky. The drizzle from two days before had returned, bringing with it a steady, unrelenting wind. "Not particularly," she drawled as she stuffed her hands into her jacket pockets and thrust out a jeans-clad hip. "Take your time. I'll search out the latest copy of *Cosmo*."

"Great," he mumbled, intent for the moment on his own thoughts.

As he dropped several coins in and began to dial, Gypsy browsed. The store was small and they were the only customers there. After asking them if they needed any help, the clerk had disappeared into the back room. He'd peek out from time to time at the unfamiliar, mismatched pair, obviously unaccustomed to strangers.

McCready, not having taken time to go to a laundry the day before, wore a light suit. The walk across the damp potato field and a misstep into a partially filled ditch had soaked the first three inches of his gray slacks, and he looked like the quintessential eastern city slicker.

Surreptitiously she looked for *World View* on the magazine rack, but it must have sold out. She settled for a copy of *Home Mechanix*, and as she flipped through it she couldn't help but hear McCready's end of the conversation. She tried to ignore it. She wouldn't even have come into town with him if she hadn't needed to stretch her legs and pick up a couple of things. As it was, the harder she tried to block out his voice, the more riveted to it she became.

"I'm calling from Wisconsin, Kevin, can you hear me okay? This connection isn't too great, it's been raining here. So, how're you doing, sport? How's your mom?"

He paused to listen and Gypsy moved closer. Evidently McCready's brand of curiosity was catching, she mused.

When he spoke again his voice had changed. "I honestly don't know, Kev. Maybe another week or so. You know I miss you too, don't you? I promise, the first weekend I'm back, we'll take off together, just the two of us. Anywhere you want, deal?"

Another pause, and Gypsy buried her face in the magazine.

McCready shifted uncomfortably on the stool, then rubbed his forehead. "Kev, I know I've broken a few promises in the past, but this time I give you my word."

Gypsy realized that she needn't have made a secret of her interest. She watched him openly now as he asked his son a series of questions about what he'd been up to, but she might as well have been invisible. McCready stared blindly out at the rain, his blue eyes mirroring the gray clouds, his expression dismal. She couldn't help but feel for his dilemma.

"An oath, huh?" he asked after a time, then chuckled. "Which oath?"

As he listened he snapped back to his surroundings, and his eyes darted to Gypsy. She pretended to be absorbed in an article on engine overhauls.

Apparently satisfied that she no longer watched,

he raised his right hand and lowered his voice. "I swear on the might of Captain Commando and the Legion of the Freedom Fighters."

Gypsy stifled a spontaneous giggle and he turned away from her view. The only thing she caught after that was his heartfelt "I love you, Kev" before he replaced the receiver.

He sat for a moment, his back to her, then stood and walked over to the comics rack. Snatching one, he held it up for her to see. *"Captain Commando's Freedom Fighters,"* he explained. "In case you were wondering."

Keane squinted in the lantern light, using his own practiced form of shorthand to take down Gypsy's words. At least this way he didn't have to worry about her deciphering the multitude of personal observations he added in the margins.

They were huddled beneath the biplane's wing, drinking lukewarm coffee. The rain had let up but it was unusually chilly for the time of year, or so he understood.

"How did your father and Neal Gallagher meet up again, and when?" he questioned between shivers. When she didn't answer him right away he raised his head. "Gypsy?"

"How old is Kevin?" she asked suddenly, startling him. She looked at him strangely, the way she had all afternoon since his call in the drug store. The light flickered in her emerald eyes and her hair clung damply about her face, its curl tightened by the humidity. Her silk scarf lay in her lap and she pulled it slowly through her fingers, then back again.

"Who's doing the interviewing here, me or you?" he joked, but he could see she waited for an answer. "He's eight," he told her.

"And he reads *Captain Commando* comic books."

Keane took a sip of his coffee, made a face, and nodded. "He's a collector. He's got at least a hundred titles, all going back to issue number one or two. When he grows up the kid'll be worth millions."

She laughed. "When did he start, at age two?"

He smiled as he remembered the day he'd entrusted the precious collection to his son. "You caught me," he confessed. "Most of the older ones are mine. Now that I don't have the time to go on collecting, Kevin's carrying on the line. He hasn't missed a number yet."

The silk scarf whisked through her long fingers. "You miss him terribly, don't you?" she asked, genuine concern in her voice.

Keane nodded again and wondered if he'd ever be able to predict the course of her thoughts. "Yes, I miss him, and I hope he knows that. I hope he doesn't blame me for missing out on half his life. His mother and I divorced when he was barely four, and I haven't been around him as much as I would've liked. It's the work—I can't stop doing it, and I don't want to. But sometimes I wonder if it'll be worth it in the long run, if I should find something more stable, with less traveling and more free time. Hell, weeks can pass and all he'll see of me is my byline. That's no way for a kid to grow up."

"Yet if you tried something else you wouldn't be happy, would you?" Gypsy countered. "And your unhappiness would affect him as much as it would you. Instead of blaming you for doing what you love to do, he'd grow up blaming himself for keeping you from it. Is that what you want for him?"

Keane felt the answer in the pit of his stomach. "My God, you could be right. I never thought about it that way. He's a sensitive little kid; do you think he'd pick up on that?"

"I know he would. I did." She looked away, her eyes focused inward. "When my father left the air circus he swore he'd go back to it as soon as he was able. But the years passed, he met my mother, and then I was born. A family is a big responsibility and he knew we could never adjust to that lifestyle, always moving, never knowing where the next meal might come from. He settled for a job as a mechanic for a major airline. I suppose he felt that just being around planes, any planes, was better than nothing. But it was a poor substitute. During the first seven years of my life I knew he was miserable. He didn't come out of it until he joined Neal again and they built Gallagher Aviation. He started to fly on a regular basis once more, and the difference in him was like night and day." She looked at Keane's pad. "I just answered your question. Aren't you going to write it down?"

He shook his head. He'd been so caught up in her words he hadn't realized they'd come full circle. He forced his pencil to move on the surface of the paper, but he was so aware of Gypsy's presence next to him he didn't even know what he was writing.

When she shivered against him he put down the pencil, took the scarf from her hands, and gently wound it about her neck. She sat stock-still while he did it, and her eyes never left his.

"Thanks," she whispered.

"Thank *you*," he answered, his voice a trifle husky. "I think you've given me enough food for thought to keep my mind whirling for a week."

She favored him with a brief smile. "It was a moment of weakness. I promise, McCready, it won't happen again."

"Don't make promises you may not be able to keep." He slowly lowered his face to hers and kissed her with the lightest of touches. She didn't slap him, and she didn't move away. So far, so good, he thought, and did it again.

Tentatively her lips began to respond beneath his, and Keane fought the sudden desire that surged through his body. *You're going to scare her off*, an inner voice warned, and sure enough, after a few more seconds she pulled away and fumbled to stand.

"Gypsy. . ."

"No." She ran her hands through her hair as she widened the distance between them. "Don't say anything else, you're confusing me."

"As far as I know, a little confusion never hurt anybody."

"You don't understand," she said from the darkness beyond the lantern.

After a weighty pause, Keane sighed. "I guess not." He could still feel the pressure of her mouth against his and he was having a hard time adjusting to her withdrawal, even though he'd seen it coming.

She stood like that for several minutes, just out

of sight and reach, before she finally said, "Go to bed, McCready, I'll be fine."

He stared at the lantern. "I know you'll be fine. And don't you think it's about time you started calling me Keane?"

A disembodied chuckle floated back to him. "Strange name," she observed.

"No more strange than yours."

She considered that in the pitch-black stillness of the night. "At least we have one thing in common."

The following day dawned sunny and warm. Keane spent the better part of it collecting money for Gypsy's rides and chatting with people when their turns were through.

As for chatting with Gypsy, they'd barely had time to say two words to each other since his aborted attempt at seduction the night before. Some finely woven thread of tension stretched between them. He could feel it. Yet he wasn't sure if he should take it to the breaking point or pull back. He'd have to go on instinct, because way out here he couldn't rely on anything else. It was as if the two of them existed in a vacuum, apart from the rest of the world. He'd never experienced a feeling quite like it.

By late afternoon he felt particularly earthbound and restless. When Gypsy taxied in from her last flight he decided to do something about it.

He sauntered up to her as she jumped from the cockpit and slowly removed her goggles and helmet. When her passenger moved out of earshot she rolled her eyes and groaned. "God, I'm tired. How much did we take in today?"

Keane's mood brightened at her use of the pronoun "we." "Exactly one hundred and four dollars," he said, showing her a wad of cash.

She groaned again. "Fifty-two rides."

They were both silent for a moment until he cleared his throat. "Uh, would you care to make that fifty-three? I've been feeling a little left out down here."

Her gloved hand went up to cover her eyes. "You've got to be kidding. Keane, I'm dead tired, and the Moth's nearly out of gas."

There. Another clue, he thought. She'd finally stopped calling him McCready. "Lame excuse," he admonished. "I helped you gas her up two rides ago, remember?"

She sagged against the fuselage. "No, no, no. I'm finished for the day and I want to take a bath in that rain water we collected. I'll take you up tomorrow —if you pay your two bucks, that is."

Keane shrugged, looked up at the sky, then shook his head. "Maybe you're right." He sighed. "My first two flights weren't great successes. Why should this one be any different? I guess you have to be a little crazy to go up in one of those things, at that. Give me a nice big seven-forty-seven any day." He continued to look at the sky as he waited. He didn't have to wait long.

"There you go, belittling the Moth again. I'll have you know, this was a perfect day for flying. The air was smooth as glass and the visibility fantastic. Look at that sunset." She pointed to the brilliant orange and pink horizon to the west. "From up there that would look like heaven. It'd be like sailing through a dream, and you'd be a first-class fool to pass up the chance."

Keane pounced. "Lord have mercy, you talked me into it. Let's go."

When she realized what he'd led her into she closed her eyes. "McCready, you are a—"

"Ah-ah-ah," he corrected. "It's Keane, remember?"

She advanced on him, hands on her slim but shapely hips, her fiery hair backlit by the setting sun. "Keane, you are a conniving, self-serving... Okay, get in the plane."

"Huh?"

"I said, get in the plane before I change my mind. You wanted a ride—you'll get one."

He assessed the gleam in her emerald eyes and wondered if he'd just made a stupid mistake.

Once they were in the air Keane forced himself to relax and concentrate on the scenery below. The earth looked like a huge patchwork quilt, all green and gold, and the surrounding lakes and ponds were blue diamonds, glistening in the now-crimson rays of the sun. The Moth glided along like a butterfly and slowly but surely it ceased to be a monstrosity to him. On the ground it was a foreign thing, a curiosity. In the air it was a beautiful machine, as much at home in the clouds as the birds.

He realized that Gypsy was taking it slow for his benefit in an attempt to let him enjoy the experience, not fear it. And it worked. When she felt he was gaining confidence she dipped into a steep glide and came down low over a miniforest of summer-green birch trees, then arched up again so that the sky filled his vision and he forgot the ground existed. When they leveled out she rolled into a sweeping turn and the blue became green as they banked to the right. This time his stomach didn't protest. This time he loved it.

He turned back to her and smiled. She nodded briefly and indicated that he should hold on. Before he realized what it was she planned they were into a complete roll and he found himself hanging upside down in the cockpit, the earth above his head. For a moment it completely disoriented him and he closed his eyes. That only made him dizzy, so he forced himself to open them and keep them open. He didn't want to miss an instant of this and he owed it to himself, and to Gypsy, not to be a coward.

After she brought the plane upright once more she further startled him by shutting down the engine, and they began a long slow glide down. The only sound Keane heard was the soft rush of wind as it played a song through the Moth's wires. About 850 feet from the ground she fired it up again and he could feel the sudden surge of power directly in front of him.

The sun had sunk below the horizon when she brought them in and taxied to a stop in the exact location they'd started from. Keane leaped out of his seat, unable to restrain a grin.

Gypsy, still seated, removed her goggles and watched him, her eyes probing.

"I feel . . ." he began. "I don't know. I guess 'free' is the word. Everything else seems so insignificant when you're up there, doesn't it?"

As if those were the very words she'd hoped to hear, Gypsy smiled. "Now you know." She jumped from the plane, the spring back in her step. "I have an idea."

"Oh?"

She pulled off her helmet and shook out her unruly auburn curls. "Let me take my bath and then we'll go into town for a real dinner, what do you say?"

Keane hesitated, expecting a catch. "You mean, you're inviting me out to dinner?"

"I know it's out of character, but that sunset did something to me, too. Better take advantage of my generosity while I'm mellow—not to mention a hundred and four dollars richer."

"I've learned it's impossible to take advantage of you, Gypsy lady," he said with a grin.

Her eyes narrowed suddenly and she backed away. "Why did you call me that?"

He shrugged and felt the grin fade. "I don't know. It seems to fit you. Don't you like it?"

"No, that's not it." She studied him for a moment, then shook herself. "Someone else used to call me that."

While she bathed behind some nearby trees Keane leaned against the warm, now-silent Moth. "There's something she hasn't told me," he mused. "She's scared, and dammit, I want to know why."

The brilliant sunset gradually turned to darkness as he kicked at a tuft of grass with his shoe. While he wasn't looking the line between the journalist and the man had blurred. In fact, there wasn't a line at all anymore. Gypsy Gallagher had erased it.

"How did you end up with the name 'Gypsy'?" Keane asked on their way back to the field at the end of the evening. The moon shone full and bright and they found their way easily.

Gypsy inhaled the fresh night air. Dinner had been an enjoyable yet baffling experience. She'd never felt truly comfortable in McCready's presence and tonight was no exception. But ever since the kiss the tone of that discomfort had changed. At the restaurant, across the table from him, she'd found herself noticing the oddest things. The way his chest rose and fell beneath his cotton shirt as he breathed. The myriad of emotions his blue eyes expressed as he told her about his work and past experiences in the journalism business. How his voice deepened when he was amused. And she'd felt that undercurrent of tension building between them like a live but unspoken presence.

She turned to him now, and a slight smile curved her lips at his question. "It took you long enough to get to that. And I thought you reporters didn't miss a trick." She gently brushed a lightning bug from her dark slacks and it took off to join its friends on the other side of a shallow ditch.

"I wanted to save it for an appropriate time," he replied, his hands deep in his pockets as he walked beside her.

"It's a nickname, really. My given name is Erin. When my father first taught me to fly he called me Gypsy, because I'd pester him with questions about his barnstorming days and scold him for not having me sooner. He told me I'd inherited the O'Hara streak of wanderlust and that I'd never be happy in one place for very long."

He chuckled. "You've fulfilled that prophecy, all

right. But in your case I wonder if wanderlust isn't just another word for running away."

He said it so casually it almost didn't register in Gypsy's mind. When it did she stopped in her tracks. "Are you going to tell me what you mean by that?" she asked quietly.

When he realized he'd left her a few paces back, he too stopped and turned. "You have to admit, it *is* convenient. You don't have to worry about relationships, because there aren't any. The only thing you have to answer to is the sky. Doesn't it get lonely, though? What do you do when you want to share a sunset with someone and there's nobody there?"

"I like what I do," she told him, and the all-too-familiar anger edged her voice like steel. But she knew the anger only served to hide the vulnerability she'd begun to feel. "Why must I always defend myself to you? What gives you the right to decide my motives?"

He moved closer. His eyes, in the moonlight, held none of the animosity she might have expected. "What do you have to defend, Gypsy?" he asked. "Your own aloneness?"

When he reached her he took hold of her shoulders and she felt an electric shock at his touch. His face was inches from hers and she willed herself not to bolt. Dear God, how could she let it happen again?

"You feel it, don't you?" he whispered.

His breath was warm on her cheek and she lowered her eyes, once, to his lips. "Yes. But that doesn't mean I want to give in to it."

"Must you always have a comeback for everything?"

"Must you always ask ridiculous questions?"

He smiled. "You're right. Let's get on with it."

His mouth found hers again and Gypsy couldn't help but respond. Something, instinct probably, moved her to take the sides of his head in her hands as the kiss deepened. Fear crept into the edges of her awareness. Fear and a warning. But she was able to hold them back as Keane awakened a flood of long-dead sensations within her.

When he slowly pulled away she opened her eyes with reluctance. The dream would have to end. Dreams always did. He was staring at her, obviously surprised by her reaction. Say something, she told herself. Don't just gaze into his eyes like a moonstruck fool. "I, uh . . ."

"My God, she's speechless."

"Keane, don't make jokes. Not now." She moved out of his grasp, needing distance.

He sighed. "Sorry. I guess I'm covering for my own lack of confidence. I feel . . . naked around you. No, wrong word, wrong word."

"Keane, please . . ."

He held up a hand. "Wait, let me finish, okay? What I should've said is I'm very attracted to you, and not just physically. I feel we've broken new ground in the last couple of days, and I don't want to jeopardize that by moving too fast."

Gypsy threw back her head and looked at the stars. "I don't believe this."

"Neither do I," he agreed. "But it's happening, nevertheless. I suggest we don't analyze it to death before it has a chance to develop."

The fear returned and this time she couldn't ignore it. Running a hand through her hair, she faced him directly. "Whatever is happening, it doesn't have a snowball's chance in hell of developing, can't you see that?"

"Why not?" he challenged. "Because you're afraid of your own feelings?"

"I'm not afraid!"

"You could have fooled me."

Frustrated, Gypsy turned and started for the plane. "I can't talk to you. We haven't been able to carry on a decent conversation since the day we met, and you still think we're compatible?"

She walked on, but he closed the distance between them in seconds. "There you go again, turning on the anger. It's a defense mechanism, just like my wisecracks. It hasn't taken me long to see through you, lady."

"Oh, and what else do you see?" she threw back over her shoulder, knowing full well she'd regret the question, because he'd answer it. She was right.

"I see that for some reason the thought of getting close to me is scaring you to death," he told her. "And for the life of me I can't figure out why."

That did it. A vital part of Gypsy's barrier against the world began to slip, and she watched it fall and shatter on the ground at Keane McCready's feet. It had taken five years to build, and only an instant to collapse. "All right! I admit it, I'm scared. Scared enough to get into the Moth and leave you right now, without looking back."

He stood silent for a moment, perplexed. Then he uttered a single word, and it hung in the air between them like a stone. "Why?"

Gypsy caught her breath. Here she was, about to spill everything she'd attempted to hide from him since the beginning, and she didn't care. The only important thing was that he understand. "Because I loved a man once. I loved him, I married him, I worked with him—and in the end I killed him."

CHAPTER
Four

KEANE FELT AS IF time had somehow stopped. Everything—breath, thought, his own heartbeat— seemed suspended as he stared at the woman before him. Even the very air surrounding them had stilled, as though it too waited.

He swallowed. "You are going to explain that statement . . . right?"

She gave her shoulders a little shrug and stepped back, out of his reach. Her eyes flicked away from his as well, toward the Moth, and he understood that the plane was an anchor of sorts for her. "You knew Neal Gallagher was my father-in-law," she said. "Why haven't you ever asked me about my marriage?"

Keane sank his hands deep in his pockets once again. "We hadn't gotten to that part of your story yet, for one thing," he told her. "And I did agree to let you direct the course of my questions. I guess I figured you'd tell me about it if and when the time was right."

She nodded and resumed her walk back to the silent biplane, her steps slow and deliberate.

Keane kept the distance she seemed to need and followed, parallel.

"Five years ago my husband Lon and I were in Blakesburg, Iowa, for the Antique Airplane Association's annual fly-in," she began. "We'd recently restored a 1931 Travel Air, and Lon wanted to show it off. Blakesburg isn't like Oshkosh. No air shows, no competitions. Just old antique aircraft buffs getting together to shoot the breeze—and fly."

Her voice softened, but Keane heard every word despite the space between them. He still wasn't accustomed to the kind of quiet a country night offered. The total absence of ordinary city sounds like traffic disoriented him.

"Our second day there Lon started to complain that the Travel Air's engine seemed to be cutting out intermittently, especially when he tried to climb. I had a look at it that evening while he went to the Pilot's Pub with a couple of friends. Everything looked fine. We'd recently replaced several original parts with rebuilt ones, and it had passed its hundred-hour inspection without a hitch." She shook her head slowly. "I tightened a couple of loose plugs I felt might be responsible for the missing, and let it go at that."

She fell silent for a few paces and Keane began to edge in closer, a bit at a time. Gypsy, her eyes on the plane, didn't notice.

"The next morning," she continued, "Lon took her up for a practice flight. I didn't go with him that time." She laughed shortly. "It's funny, but now I don't even remember what my reasons were. Instead, I watched from in front of the aviation museum. It happened on his third pass over the field. Because I'd okayed the plane he decided to put her through some maneuvers. It was early yet and the sky was his. After a few rolls he started to climb. I was wondering if he planned to try a hammerhead when the engine began to sputter. I . . ." She swallowed convulsively and closed her eyes, coming to a halt several yards from the Moth. "It cut out altogether before he'd gained enough altitude to be able to pull out of a full spin, or even glide to the runway. He came in nose down and far too fast, then hit like a stone. Lon was probably already dead before the fire started . . . In any case, I couldn't get to him."

"Oh, God," Keane groaned as he remembered with crystal clarity the Stearman's accident at Oshkosh. No wonder she'd been so shaken by it. He'd managed to bridge the distance between Gypsy and himself by half, but he didn't dare move any closer now.

After she took in a deep breath, her voice sank to a near-whisper. "A lot of the engine was salvageable. The FAA investigated and eventually found the cause of the engine failure. It seemed the fuel pump had developed a hairline crack, which allowed gas to escape. When Lon went into that steep climb the crack gave and it split apart."

"Couldn't it have cracked on impact?" Keane asked.

"Unlikely. The only other explanation would have been pilot error, and everyone who knew Lon knew better. He was an excellent flier and he'd done that stunt at least a thousand times. He'd never have let her stall only a third of the way up. It'd be like a college student suddenly forgetting how to spell."

"So you blame yourself, is that it?"

She turned to look at him for the first time since her narrative began and the moonlight found traces of tears on her cheeks. "I was negligent." She said it flatly, without emotion. "If I'd looked more carefully I might have seen it, don't you understand? Lon trusted me with his life that day and I let him down . . ."

"The hell you did." Keane gave in to his urge to go to her. If she wanted to run, fine, but where could she go in an empty potato field? Taking hold of her shoulders, he shook her, hard. "Who else blamed you besides yourself, Gypsy? The FAA? Your father-in-law? Did anyone actually say it?"

Angry, she struggled to free herself.

"Dammit, look at me! You say your husband trusted you with his life. Then give him a little credit, for crying out loud; he must have had reason to. If you're half as good a mechanic as people say you are, you wouldn't have let anything get by you."

"You just don't get it, do you?"

"Oh, so now *I'm* the idiot."

They stared at one another, breathing hard, until Gypsy managed to wrench herself from his hold.

Keane clenched his fists as she turned her back on him again. Somewhere along the line his sympathy for her had changed to frustrated anger. After a moment he raised his arms and shouted to the vast empty field, "What we have here, ladies and gentlemen of Libertyville, is one Erin Gypsy Gallagher, self-appointed saint and guardian of the human race. Ex-angel, that is. You see, she quit that particular job when she realized she wasn't omnipotent. Quit outright and took to the sky where she really belongs . . . eyes on the clouds and don't look down, isn't that right, Gypsy? Because you might fall from grace if you look down, won't you? Just like the first time."

She stood rigid by the tail of the Moth.

Overhead a star shot from the sky, curving in a swift arc to who knew where.

"How poetic," Keane muttered. "She even generates her own special effects." Cautious, he came up behind her and gently touched her hair.

To his surprise she slumped, head lowered.

"Gypsy." He said it tentatively. "Look, I'm sorry, but—"

"Maybe I deserve it," she murmured.

"Maybe you do." Keane steeled himself and turned her to face him.

She didn't bother to hide her tears. She merely gazed at him, unblinking, as he moved closer and took her into his arms.

At first she stiffened, but when he only rested his chin on top of her head and sighed, she began to relax. He held her that way for a time and tried not to make any sudden, unexpected moves.

After several minutes passed her hands slowly encircled his waist. Her touch was pure gratifying flame, and Keane closed his eyes against the power of his own desire for her.

In a way, it was funny. Her strength had been her first quality to attract him. It had made the chase worthwhile. Now her present vulnerability threatened to undo him completely.

By degrees he lowered his head until he was again looking into her tear-shimmered green eyes. "Whatever happened, however it happened, you weren't the one who died that day, Gypsy," he whispered as he stroked her moist cheeks with his thumbs. "You're as alive as I am, right here and right now. Let me prove it to you."

Gypsy leaned into his embrace as Keane's lips closed over hers in a hesitant, slightly salty kiss.

She didn't want to think anymore tonight. She was as far past thought as she'd ever been, and it wasn't nearly the weightless, stomach-churning drop she'd feared. Only Keane's words continued to echo through her mind as she willingly deepened the kiss, holding him with all the strength she possessed.

"You're alive..."

For the first time in five years she knew it was true.

Once unleashed, the passion between them became a live thing, a force neither of them could, or even wanted to, control. Somehow Keane managed to drag her sleeping bag from the plane and spread it beneath the wing without breaking contact. Then he lowered her gently onto it as his lips sought and found the sensitive hollow of her throat.

Gypsy closed her eyes and savored the heat his mouth brought to her skin. It was as though every inch of her body was electrified, waiting only for his touch.

His strong hands parted her blouse, but before he removed it entirely he paused. "Are you sure?" he asked, his voice made husky by desire.

She nodded and pulled him back to her. "Don't talk," she whispered. "Just love me."

He groaned at her words, and Gypsy soon discovered that flight had its equal on the earth. They finished undressing one another with feverish urgency, and the mild night air kissed her skin where Keane's own warm flesh hadn't already seared it.

She marveled at the harmony they were able to create together and arched with pleasure at the forcefulness of his body. Lean and muscular, it melded with the contours of her own, as though they were two interlocking pieces of the same wonderful puzzle.

She took what he offered her, giving herself in return, and for a time the world went away.

When it came back they lay together in contentment, arms and legs intertwined. Keane's tousled head rested on her shoulder and Gypsy ran her fingers through the soft golden-brown strands of his hair.

He sighed, and his breath sent a thrill over her sensitized nerve endings. "You are so beautiful, my green-eyed gypsy," he said. "I—"

Quickly she moved her fingers to his lips. "Shhh. I don't want to think, I just want to feel."

"But—"

"Please, Keane."

He raised himself to one elbow and looked at her in the waning moonlight. A frown tugged at the corners of his lips but he respected her wishes and said nothing more.

Gypsy reached up to trace the curve of his cheek as his gaze wandered down over her body stretched beside him. His breath began to quicken and she smiled, drawing him to her once again.

This time the love they made was slow and sensuous, lacking the urgency of their first tumultuous encounter. With the joyful innocence of a child,

Gypsy let herself discover the man that was Keane McCready. Just as he had opened new avenues of sensation for her, she sought and found his special areas of pleasure and awakened them one by one, gratified by each success.

It had been good with Lon, but never like this. This was special. Special in a way she'd never dreamed was possible, and when at last they neared exhausted sleep in one another's arms, a single tear for the past escaped her closed eyes.

Perhaps, after all, there could be a future.

Keane stirred, locked in an unsettling dream.

He and Gypsy were high in the air above a story-book farm community. The sky was vivid cobalt blue and Gypsy was pushing him out onto the bottom wing of the Moth.

"Wait!" he shouted over the roar of the wind and the biplane's engine. "Can't we talk this over some more, my little Snoopyette, my darling Gypsy-cakes?"

She laughed as she banked to the left over a picturesque lake.

Keane covered his eyes, one foot on the wing, the other in the forward cockpit. He held on for dear life.

"You knew what you were getting into when we began this 'partnership,'" she reminded him. "I call the shots, remember? Now, get out on that wing, sweet-cheeks."

"But, honeybuns . . ."

With a swift shove, she forced him out onto its slippery surface.

Several hundred feet below them a crowd had

gathered around a little farmhouse. Possessing the
uncanny senses of a dreamer, Keane could hear
them talking excitedly amongst themselves as he
crouched, hands clenched in a death grip around the
wing struts. "Now what?" he shouted.

"You're a wing walker, dear," Gypsy replied. "So
start walking, or you won't get your portion of beef
stew for dinner tonight."

As the wind whipped at his hair and clothing
Keane slowly stood. "Oh, God," he groaned when
the Moth dipped. "I wish I were back in Afghani-
stan, tooling around in that open Jeep . . ."

In a twinkling they were on the ground once
more. The enthusiastic crowd had surrounded
Gypsy and she basked in their admiration. Her
boots were polished to a high sheen and her silk
scarf blew out in a perfect arc behind her dust-free
auburn hair.

Keane picked a bug from between his teeth and
watched from the sidelines.

"Oh, it was nothing, really," Gypsy was saying.
"But come back next week. My partner will eject
himself from the cockpit and land on a minitrampo-
line on top of that barn over there."

Keane's eyes widened at that. Then he forced
himself to stifle a groan as Paul Daniels and the
great T. C. Bitteman stepped from the crowd to approach him.

Daniels stuffed a dollar bill into Keane's shirt
pocket and clapped him on the back. "Congratula-
tions, McCready, and keep up the good work.
That's one hell of a talented employer you've got
there."

"Photogenic, too," Bitteman added.

"She's my wife," Keane told them. "My little Red Baroness, my darling prop jockey..."

"Whatever..."

Gypsy heard Keane moan in his sleep, but she was too drowsy to respond. The unaccustomed feel of his strong body next to her was comforting, yet distracting at the same time.

She shifted atop the sleeping bag as a dream took hold of her awareness...

"Honey, did you remember to pack my green-and-yellow striped tie—the one little Erin sprayed oatmeal on the last time I was here in April?"

Gypsy made her ponderous way across their cramped New York City apartment to where Keane stood, suitcase in hand, ready to embark on yet another assignment for his magazine.

"I'm afraid the stain didn't come out, dear," she told him. "But I bought another one just like it. I walked all over Manhattan the other day until I found the exact colors."

Keane smiled and patted her on the head, then winced as one of her hair rollers pricked his finger. "You know you shouldn't be exerting yourself now, hon. The baby's due any moment."

She shrugged. "All for a worthy cause. Besides, you know how I like to stay on the move. You will check in from time to time, won't you, darling? So you'll know whether to bring home a voodoo doll with pink feathers or blue?"

He looked at her in surprise. "Sweetheart, the jungles of North Africa aren't exactly littered with phone booths."

"I know." She sighed. "But I was so hoping..."

"Chin up, old girl. Once I fly into New Delhi next week, I promise to mail you a postcard."

From the back bedroom came the patter of little feet as Keane Jr. ran to Gypsy, a model biplane in one outstretched hand. "Ma, you said you'd help me with the nose gear. Oh, hi, Dad. When did you get home?"

Gypsy stooped awkwardly and took the boy's shoulders. "He came in for a pit stop last night, but I'm afraid he has to leave again this morning."

Keane reached down to pat his youngest son's sandy head. "I'll see you in a couple of weeks, uh . . ."

"Keane Jr.," Gypsy finished.

"Right. You have a good time at school today, big fella."

"But Dad, it's summer vacation." He turned back to Gypsy. "Ma, did you really used to fly one of these back in the olden days?"

Keane hefted his suitcase as a fond smile touched his lips. "You should have seen her, son. What a character—doing those lazy eights and barrel rolls —making me sick left and right. Of course, all things must come to an end, isn't that right, Mrs. McCready?"

"But why? Why did she have to stop?"

Gypsy tried to get to her feet, but failed until Keane hoisted her up with a grunt. "Why did I stop?" she repeated, then shook her head as she gazed at the white silk napkins she'd fashioned from her old scarf, lying on the kitchen table. One was soaked in pancake syrup. "I . . . don't really know. Why *did* I stop, Keane? Why . . . ?"

Why . . . why . . . why?

* * *

She awoke with a start to find Keane watching her as he made coffee on the little tin stove.

"Bad dream?" he asked.

Gypsy rubbed her eyes and brushed back her hair. "No, uh . . . that is, I don't remember."

He nodded and returned his attention to the coffee, but not before an odd expression flitted across his face. "Gypsy-cakes?" he murmured.

"Pardon?"

He gave his head a slight shake. "Oh, nothing. I was just wishing we had some nice fat pancakes for breakfast, that's all."

"Pancakes?" Gypsy's eyes narrowed. "With white silk napkins?"

"Huh?"

She stood abruptly, wrapping their thin blanket around her body as she did so. It seemed no matter what she did, she couldn't avoid those probing blue eyes of his.

He finished with the coffee and held a cup out to her. He of course was fully dressed, except for his shoes.

When she reached for it he caught her hand and pulled her down beside him. "Gypsy, you don't . . . regret last night, do you?" he asked softly.

She shrugged off the last vestiges of the dream and smiled. "No, Keane, I don't regret last night," she told him, then leaned over and placed a light kiss on the side of his mouth.

He sighed and held her close. "You had me worried for a minute there. My self-confidence isn't at its strongest when I'm with you."

"Keep you hopping, do I?" She smiled against his cheek.

"That about says it."

After a moment she pulled away. "I do want you to know that I don't take what happened lightly."

"Neither do I . . ."

Gypsy pressed two fingers to his lips. He must understand. "Let me say this, okay?"

Silent, he nodded.

"This was the first time," she began, "that I've made love with a man since Lon died, and I'm not sure of my feelings yet. I don't want a summer fling . . ."

"Hey, hey . . . my turn, Gypsy lady." He looked her directly in the eye and his voice was firm. "This is not a 'fling,' all right? Let's get that straight right now."

"But—"

"No buts." He cupped her chin in his palms and she felt a rush of warmth pass from his body and into hers. "I think what we both need to do is just relax and see where it takes us." He laughed weakly. "In some ways I'm as scared as you, so don't think you're the only one who has something at stake."

Gypsy took a deep breath. "There is one point we need to address."

"What is it?"

He looked wary, but she had no choice. The question had to be asked. "What I told you last night . . . about Lon. It's off the record, Keane."

He stared at her in befuddlement for a long moment. Then he blinked and ran one hand across his face.

"Please."

His sudden laugh seemed to echo in the empty field. "Oh, this is precious. Do you know that for the first time in I don't know how long, I actually forgot I was a journalist. You made me forget. I woke up this morning and I was a man, Gypsy. A man who'd just shared a beautiful night with a very special woman. And I'll tell you something, it felt good. But I see you haven't forgotten anything, have you?"

Gypsy clutched the blanket more tightly about her. "I'm sorry, but I had to be sure."

"Oh, you can be sure, all right." He stood with his coffee. "My God, can't you get it through your head that I'm not out to hurt you? What do I have to do to prove it?"

She said nothing. What *could* she say? She'd hurt his pride, or his sense of ethics, or maybe just his feelings. She had her answer, nonetheless. But at what cost?

When she remained silent he sighed and shuffled his feet. "I can see this relationship is getting off to a rip-roaring start. I can't wait to find out what happens next."

Surprisingly, Keane found his bewildered anger hard to shake. Surprising because he was rarely one to hold a grudge, and because he would much rather have spent their remaining time in Liberty-ville on Gypsy's good side.

As it was, she'd decided to cross over into Illinois a day sooner than originally planned. In the Moth, high above and far away from the place they'd made love, neither one of them need speak.

They flew in low over the golden corn fields of Ashford Grove late on a Saturday afternoon. Gypsy had friends there and soon she and Keane found themselves enjoying country fried chicken and mountains of mashed potatoes at the farm couple's kitchen table.

"McCready," Gene Williams mused after Gypsy explained Keane's presence. "McCready, yeah. I've read your stuff. Very incisive. You're a square shooter, rare in that kind of business."

Keane eyed the man over his corn on the cob. Lean-faced and ascetic-looking, he seemed somehow out of his element. "Thanks. And pardon me for saying, but you don't look like a farmer."

Williams laughed. "Oh, and what is a farmer supposed to look like?"

Linda, his tiny-boned blond wife, traded smiles with Gypsy. "Actually, we're from Milwaukee," she told Keane. "We've always wanted to live closer to nature, so we bought this land a couple of years ago and said good-bye to the hustle and bustle."

"Quite a step in this economy."

"Maybe. But we're determined to make it work."

"Mmm-hmm." Keane suddenly became aware that Gypsy was watching him. She hadn't said much during the entire meal, and her emerald eyes were pensive as she followed his and Linda's exchange.

The little farmhouse was modest, but clean and homey. The Williamses had offered them rooms for the night, yet Keane was beginning to feel a little claustrophobic. As Gene and Linda reminisced about their high school days in Milwaukee, his own mind couldn't help but spiral back to the night he and Gypsy shared beneath the biplane's wing. She'd been so open to him, so lacking in inhibitions. Every smooth inch of her body had been a challenge to him, and her every movement a delight. Damn, why was he behaving like such an ass?

"Gypsy," Linda was saying, "do you remember that time in the tenth grade when we ditched class to spend the day at the lake? And you got so sunburned I practically had to carry you home."

Gypsy nodded absently. "I remember." For some reason it was difficult for her to keep her eyes off Keane. Now that she could observe him in the company of others he seemed somehow different. An odd feeling of jealousy passed through her and she frowned when she realized that she didn't want to share him with anybody. Time had become precious, and though she didn't regret seeking out her old friends, she wished she could think of an excuse to cut the visit short.

She watched, fascinated, as he laughed at some joke or another of Gene's. Why hadn't she noticed the brilliance of his smile before, or the way his eyes seemed to change color with his mood? Was it because she'd been so wrapped up in her own past, and her ever-present fears? She had to admit, the fears were ebbing a bit. Not entirely, but a bit. And in their place came a new willingness to explore the sensations Keane had awakened in her.

They'd hardly spoken two words to each other all day. Her original plan was to use Gene and Linda as a buffer between them while they sorted out their thoughts. Now, however, she could see it wasn't working. At least not for her.

She nudged her mind back on track when she realized someone had asked her a question. "What? I'm sorry, I guess I was daydreaming."

"I just asked you what Neal was up to these days," Gene repeated.

"Ah." She took in a deep breath, then lied. "The same old thing, really. Work, work, work."

Keane leveled a speculative glance her way.

"Doesn't that man ever take any time off?" Linda asked as she served a scrumptious dessert of strawberries and whipped cream.

Gypsy picked up her spoon and swirled it around in the smooth topping. It reminded her of a cloud seen from above, a soft cotton-candy pillow in a midsummer blue sky. "You know Neal," she answered. "His work is his pleasure. Why take a vacation from something you love?"

"I suppose you're right. Give him our best when you see him."

"I will." Keane was just about to pop a ripened strawberry into his mouth when she caught his eye. He paused, and the very corner of his lip twitched upward in an involuntary smile before he looked away. Ah-ha! she thought. A crack in the armor of wounded pride.

"So, how long are you planning to fly out of Ashford Grove?" Gene asked Gypsy through a mouthful of fruit.

She cocked her head as though she were a thousand miles away, then murmured, "Yes, it's delicious, thank you."

Keane blinked. What in the world was going on in the woman's head? A soft smile curved her lips as she continued to play with her dessert. She had yet to sample a bite.

"Uh, a couple of days, I think," he covered for her swiftly.

Gene nodded and glanced at his wife, who shrugged.

Keane's claustrophobia was getting worse by the moment. The tension between himself and Gypsy had become almost palpable and every time he looked at her he had to suppress an overwhelming urge to laugh. It wasn't an uncommon sensation. He'd had the feeling before, sometimes during interviews with ultraserious politicians. When he was a kid he'd had to clamp his hand over his mouth in church. Stately dinner parties were also fertile ground, but here? Now?

He stood abruptly. "I, uh, need to get some air."

"I'll go with you," Gene offered. "I could do with a cigarette, and Linda doesn't like me smoking in the house."

Keane forced himself not to look at Gypsy on their way out, and when at last they stepped onto the front porch he released an explosive giggle.

Gene watched him.

"I'm sorry," Keane apologized when he could.

"That's okay." After he'd lit up, the other man faced him squarely. "This may be none of my business, and you can tell me to butt out if you want, but do you and Gypsy have something going?"

The question didn't surprise Keane. "It's that obvious, huh?"

Gene laughed. "The way you two were looking at each other in there didn't leave much to the imagination."

The sun had gone down and Keane lifted his face to the cool breeze. Crickets sang in nearby bushes and he felt the knot in his stomach slowly loosen.

They stood quietly for several minutes, enjoying

the fresh air, and when Gene spoke again his voice had turned somber. "Gypsy means a great deal to us, Keane. We all go back a long way, and we wouldn't want to see her hurt."

"What makes you think I'd hurt her?" Keane asked. He was getting sick and tired of defending himself when he hadn't done anything.

Gene rested his foot on the porch railing and studied him. "She's told you about her husband, hasn't she?"

"Yeah."

"Lon was my best friend, so I know how much those two meant to one another. The truth is, I'm not sure Gypsy's ever gotten over his death."

"She has to let go of the past sometime, and I think she's already taken the first steps."

"Because of you?"

Keane nodded. "Yes, because of me."

Gene took a long slow drag from his cigarette as he considered that. "Then the only advice I can give you is to take it very easy. Do you have the time, though?"

Do I have the time? Keane asked himself. Or am I reaching for something I wasn't meant to have? "I care very much for her," he said softly. "And whatever happens, I'll do my best not to hurt her. But I think she's stronger than you realize. I think she's stronger than even *she* realizes."

"McCready, my man, for your sake and hers, I hope you're right."

"Keane is an incredibly attractive man," Linda said as she cleared the kitchen table. "Are you in love with him by any chance?"

Gypsy scalded her tongue on a sip of hot coffee. She set the cup down with a thud. *"What?"*

"You heard me just fine, and you're dying to tell me. Otherwise why would you have brought him here?"

"I think I brought him here so we wouldn't be alone together tonight."

Linda stopped clearing and sat. "That's an admission if ever I heard one. And you brought him here to see if we liked him, right?"

Gypsy stared at her friend. "Are you saying that I'm seeking your approval or something?"

"Why not? You can't bring him home to mother, so I don't mind playing the next best thing."

"This is ridiculous. It's my life; I don't need anyone's approval." Gypsy stood and paced the small kitchen, suddenly restless.

"Then why aren't you out there in the boonies with him right now? Don't think I didn't notice those sparks during dinner."

"All right, I give up! Yes, I'm attracted to him. Yes, I might even be a little in love with him, but I have no idea where it might lead."

"My God. You mean you're finally ready to put Lon to rest?"

It wasn't as though she hadn't asked herself that question at least a hundred times. Maybe now it was time she answered it. "I'm scared," she admitted. "I swore to myself that I never wanted to be that vulnerable again. When you love someone, you give them the power to take everything away."

"I've been down that road myself, you know," Linda reminded her. "But if you don't take the risk sometime, can you truly say you're a part of the human race? If you feel this strongly for him, I say go for it. Not many people are lucky enough to find that kind of love twice in a lifetime."

"But how do I know if it's that kind of love?"

"If it's right, you'll know it."

Gypsy smiled. "How did you get so wise, anyway? We're practically the same age."

Linda shrugged.

While Gypsy was still lost in thought against a kitchen counter, Keane and Gene sauntered in from the porch. Cautiously she lifted her eyes to Keane's mercurial blue ones. They stared at one another for a long moment, then Keane's lips began to twitch. Gypsy felt a giggle coming on herself, and she didn't even try to hold it back.

They both erupted at the same time. Soon Gene and Linda joined in, unable to keep straight faces themselves.

Once their laughathon was over Gypsy sensed a difference in the air. All the built-up tension was gone, and in its place was a comfortable kind of pleasure.

"Well, you still want to use those rooms?" Linda asked.

Gypsy glanced at Keane.

He looked back, one eyebrow raised.

"No," she decided. "I think we'll go back to the plane."

The smile of relief he gave her was almost worth all the hours of confusion.

CHAPTER
Five

KEANE AWOKE THE NEXT morning as a warm, moist kiss was planted on his bare shoulder. He smiled drowsily but didn't open his eyes, content to drift with the memory of last night's lovemaking. "Mmm, you're insatiable, you know that?" he murmured as the kiss traveled down his arm. When it reached the inside of his elbow he giggled. "Gypsy, that tickles, come on."

A low snort was his only answer.

"Are you catching cold, my little green-eyed temptress? I warned you about that cool night air." He raised his hand to draw her down beside him, but instead of the smooth skin he expected, he felt coarse, wiry fur and the tip of a very pointed ear. His lids snapped open and his heart skipped a few beats. Staring down at him with a kind of complacent curiosity was one of the most repulsive creatures he'd ever seen. Its wide pink snout twitched as it sensed his shock and it let out another disgusting snort.

Keane sat up with a cry, but when he tried to extricate himself from the sleeping bag it tangled around his hips and he fell back, trapped.

"Say 'bologna,'" came Gypsy's voice from a few

feet away as she snicked off some shots with his Nikon. She was fully dressed in jeans and a red T-shirt stenciled with the words GALLAGHER AVIA-TION.

Keane gritted his teeth and gave her a frozen smile as he inched away from the huge pink monster. His back came up against the edge of the Moth's bottom wing. "Will you please get this... animal away from me?"

"He's only a hog. He won't hurt you. He must have wandered here from somebody's pasture."

The creature took a step toward him.

Keane stifled a moan. "Gypsy, for God's sake, he's drooling. I think for once it's the bacon that wants *me* for breakfast."

Gypsy sighed and lowered the camera. "Oh, very well," Calmly she approached the hog. "Party's over, Henry. Time to run along home. Go on, shoo!"

After one more hungry look at Keane, it turned and trotted off through the fallow corn field they'd chosen to fly out of.

"That has to be the biggest porker I've ever seen in my life," Keane said when his heart started up again. He turned to Gypsy. "You took *pictures*?"

She shrugged. "I figured I could always use something to blackmail you with if I ever got desperate."

Backlit by a cloudless blue sky, her lightly freckled face glowing with vitality, she was a vision. Even in grubbies, without a speck of makeup, she looked sexier to him than all the women he'd ever known put together.

Keane laughed weakly and extended his hand. "Give me the camera, Gypsy."

She shook her auburn head and winked. "Uh-uh. If you want it, you're going to have to untangle yourself from that bag and come get it."

He glanced around for his pants. Last night they'd been so eager to taste one another again that they'd both let their clothes lay where they fell. Now everything was gone.

As he began to understand what she had on her sneaky little mind she favored him with a tantalizing grin.

"You've turned into one wicked lady," he marveled, then returned her smile with one of his own. "I love it."

"Your pants are in the forward cockpit. Care to guess how many pictures I can take before you reach them?"

Keane's smile faded somewhat when he remembered the Nikon had a fresh roll of film in it, but he refused to be intimidated. The humiliation he'd suffered because of that overgrown pig was bad enough. Photos of him running around a corn field in the buff would only add insult to injury. On the other hand, he didn't have a whole lot of options.

Sooner than she might have expected he pulled himself free and sprinted for the cockpit. As promised, his clothes were there. He tried not to hear the repeated click of the camera's shutter while he struggled into his trousers. "I'm gonna get you for this, my wild Irish rose," he muttered.

"You think *Playgirl* would buy these?" she asked, backing away from him.

Keane forgot about his shirt and shoes and made

a mad lunge for her, but she was fast. Like a shot she was halfway across the field, heading for a sea of eight-foot corn stalks on the other side.

"If that's the way she wants to play it ..." He dashed after her, but with bare feet it was slow going, and by the time he made the adjoining field she was out of sight. He came to a halt and bent to catch his breath. Several moments passed in which he heard only the rustling of the corn stalks in the morning breeze. Then he heard a noise to his right and saw a flash of color. He began to smile. "I've got you now, babe. You may have no equals in the air, but on the ground it's my party."

Swiftly he bridged the distance and made a flying leap, intending to bring her down beneath him. Shades of Oshkosh, he thought in the split second before he hit. He knew it wasn't her the moment he made contact, but it was too late to stop. His hands closed around cloth-encased straw and he found himself nose to nose with a carrot all the way to the ground.

Adrenaline pumping, he rolled off his lifeless prey to the further sound of the clicking camera.

A scarecrow.

Gypsy emerged from behind a stalk, wearing an ear-to-ear grin. "Got you that time, didn't I, McCready?"

Keane thought fast. Pulling the carrot from the scarecrow's comical face, he tossed it to her. "Catch!"

Before her mind could register the trick, instinct took over and she let the Nikon fall as her hands made a grab for it.

Keane dived and caught the camera in the nick of

time. "I told you," he said, smiling up at her. "On the ground it's my party."

She chuckled, conceding defeat. "In that case, am I invited? Or is three a crowd?"

"Don't worry. If he comes nosing around my territory I'll pull his eyes out. Get down here."

She knelt beside him and this time he didn't leave anything to chance. In one swift move he straddled her body with his. She could have resisted, but she didn't.

"Oh, yes," he sighed. "Much more like it."

"You mean you'd rather have me in your arms than a hog or a scarecrow?"

Keane traced her lips with his fingertips. He found it difficult to talk all of a sudden. "No contest," he whispered.

She took his hand and placed a light kiss in the center of his palm, then drew him down. "Then we're both winners."

"I'd say so."

Gypsy was dipping low over the same corn field later that afternoon when a dull orange Waco buzzed the Moth, nearly sending her into a tailspin as she fought the resultant turbulence.

Her passenger, who just happened to be the Williamses' seventy-two-year-old handyman, turned to her with a grin and shouted, "Dogfight!"

Unable to share his enthusiasm, Gypsy allowed the Moth to ride a sudden downdraft, then leveled out, her heart thumping. The other biplane had come up behind them, seemingly from nowhere. Now it circled back, and any doubts she might have had about the buzz being purposeful were dashed. It fully intended to do it again.

When the Moth felt steady enough Gypsy gritted her teeth and pulled back on the stick. In an instant the ground fell away and they began a steep climb, leaving the Waco well below. The sun, still high in the sky, glinted off the Moth's wing tips as they pushed toward the apex of an invisible roller coaster. She topped it out at twenty-five hundred feet, and for a moment felt that familiar sensation of weightlessness, as though they were balanced on the head of a pin. How many angels? she thought before she eased the stick forward, pointing the biplane's nose once more toward earth.

The Waco was still trying to climb as the Moth dived. Before its pilot could react, Gypsy had already pulled out at the bottom. The small knot of people in the field scattered when she made her final approach, confused as to what had just happened. Less than a minute had passed since the Waco made its appearance.

With a gentle flair she set the Moth down, then taxied to a complete stop. High overhead, the other biplane began its own descent.

"Holy cats!" cried the elderly handyman as he scrambled from the front cockpit to meet his friends. "Did you all see that? The lady's an *ace*!"

Gypsy cut the engine and sat still, eyes closed behind her goggles. But a strong pair of male hands on her shoulders shook her back to reality a bit too soon and she opened them again to focus on Keane's anxious face.

"Are you okay?" he asked.

With an effort, she nodded. "Fine." Slowly she

removed the goggles and her helmet, then looked around. "Where is he?"

Reassured by the edge in her voice, Keane pointed to the other side of the field. "Just coming in over there. What the hell did that maniac think he was doing?"

"I don't know, but I mean to find out."

He followed her as she strode across the field. "By the way, that was a neat trick."

"Why not? It worked with a carrot and a camera, after all."

The Waco met them halfway as it taxied in. It was an old machine, early-twenties vintage, Gypsy guessed, and it showed its age. No wonder it hadn't been able to keep up with her.

Its pilot, a tall husky youth, pulled himself from the single cockpit and removed his own goggles.

Unbelievable, she thought. He can't be much more than seventeen years old!

His size didn't deter Keane. Before Gypsy had gotten over her surprise he had the kid by the shirt-front, back against the fuselage. "Whatever your explanation is, it's not going to be good enough, but I'll listen anyway, *then* tear your head off."

Gypsy watched, stunned, as the boy sized up his opponent, then slowly raised his hands in defeat. Something glittered in Keane's eyes. Something she'd never seen there before. A hard-edged anger that evidently warned the young pilot not to test his luck.

"Talk to me," he demanded.

"Hey, ease up, I was just horsing around. Look, my name's Roger Corman; I do a lot of crop dusting around here."

Keane didn't ease up, nor did his eyes lose that strange glitter. "Okay, Roger Corman, tell me something else. Are you aware you could have killed somebody up there?"

By now the crowd had surrounded the Waco, looking on with an unvoiced but very real excitement. Gypsy could feel the tension in the air. So, they saw it, too.

"I wouldn't have hurt anybody..." the boy began.

When it looked as though Keane was about to haul off and punch him, Gypsy stepped forward. "Keane, let him go."

At first she thought he hadn't heard her; then his eyes cleared and he slowly released the youth and took a step back.

Gypsy forced herself to turn and look at the other pilot. "Are you licensed to fly this?"

"Sure I am. I've logged almost two hundred hours. What do you take me for?"

"An idiot. If I'd pulled a stunt like that when I was your age, my father would've disowned me. Then again, when I was your age, I'd logged over a thousand hours. Enough to know better."

The boy looked her up and down in disbelief, his eyes narrowed. "That was *you* up there?"

"No, it was Lindbergh's ghost." She started to walk away, then turned back. "You keep your distance from this field, and my plane, for the next two days, Roger, or I'll buy this Waco from whoever you work for, then burn it myself. Along with your license."

"But I was told to find..."

Gypsy didn't stick around to hear the rest. She

strode back to the Moth and busied herself looking for her tool box. After the workout she'd just given the engine it was about time to check the cylinder base nuts to see if they needed tightening. She also needed to cool off, and she sure as hell wasn't about to hop any more rides until Roger, the flying boy wonder, was long gone from the field.

She glanced once at the Waco as she climbed up onto the Moth's cowling. The kid was still talking to Keane. The handyman and his fellow onlookers, obviously disappointed that their confrontation hadn't erupted into violence, were scattering.

Would Keane have hit the boy if she hadn't intervened? She didn't know. She honestly didn't know. The fact surprised her and she frowned. How well did she know him? How well could anyone truly know another person in such a relatively short time? And yet here she was, falling for the man as fast as she'd just sailed down from the sky. How long before she either hit the ground or pulled out?

The sun, hot on her back, made her realize she'd been staring at him for several minutes. He was reading a small piece of paper the boy handed him, but she was too far away to gauge his expression. He nodded, then started in her direction as the young pilot replaced his goggles and climbed up into the Waco.

Gypsy quickly lowered her head and got to work. When Keane sauntered up to stand by the prop a few moments later, she pretended to be absorbed in her task.

"Well," he said, "you certainly told him what for, didn't you?"

She shrugged and attacked a loose nut with a zeal

she didn't quite feel. "I thought maybe he should live to see eighteen."

"What's that supposed to mean?"

The question sounded so innocently curious that she shook her head and sighed. "We're going to need gas. Want to flip to see who goes?"

"Uh, I'll go. Maybe I can hitch a ride with Claude, the handyman." He gathered up several gas cans and started across the field, toward the road where a few cars and trucks were still parked. Once, he paused to look back at her, opened his mouth to say something, then changed his mind and kept on.

Gypsy laid down her wrench and removed her jacket as the Waco finally took off, passing overhead before it veered sharply left, on its way to town.

"Maybe it's time I asked you a couple of more questions, Mr. Wordsmith," she mused. "Before you blind me completely."

"Why did your marriage break up?"

Keane choked on a bite of cold pizza. *"What?* Where did that come from?"

Gypsy was stretched out on top of the sleeping bag, one long, jeans-clad leg crossed over the other, playing with her scarf again. "Call it . . . idle curiosity. That, and making conversation. You haven't been your usual talkative self this evening."

Keane realized he didn't really want the pizza anyway and tossed the remainder of his slice into the box, which lay between them. The stars and moon were so bright they almost didn't need the lantern to see each other. Its wavering orange hue sent shadows chasing over Gypsy's face, making it impossible to read. Oh, but she looked lovely, though. He fought an urge to reach out and trace the hollow of her throat with his fingertips, to follow it down to her breastbone, and beyond. "I . . . I, uh, guess my mind's been somewhere else. Sorry."

"I guess it has."

He pulled in a deep breath and sat up straighter. "Why did my marriage break up? You want the official version, or the truth?"

"Which is better?"

"They're both pretty much the same, with one slight difference. My career, the hours, the traveling. The arguments over the career, the hours, and the traveling. In the public version Beth got fed up and couldn't take it anymore, so she left." He rubbed at his eyes and chuckled. "The truth is, we'd become strangers to one another a long time before. She only stayed around as long as she did for Kevin's sake. When the arguments started to affect him we both decided he'd be better off if we called it quits. Divorce may be hard on kids, but sometimes seeing parents constantly at each other's throats can be worse."

"I'm sorry," Gypsy said softly.

"Don't be. We all have our problems. That's what life's all about, right? Having been married yourself, I'm sure you know how it is."

"Come again?"

He blinked. "Oh, don't tell me you and Lon never fought. It's an obligatory part of the institution, isn't it? I mean, look at us. We've only just started this relationship and we've hardly done anything else."

"Lon and I had a wonderful marriage. There wasn't any room in it for foolish bickering."

Her tone seemed genuine enough, but he knew she had to be kidding. "Oh yeah? Then there probably wasn't room in it for much juice either, was there?"

She looked away from him and went back to playing with her scarf. "I'm not sure I like where this is going."

"You started it, remember?" Keane leaned back on his elbows as little wheels began to turn in his mind. "I think ... no, I really do believe I've got you figured now."

"I'm glad one of us can say that."

"Gypsy, I'm serious, this is a real breakthrough for me. Now I understand."

"Understand *what*, for God's sake?"

"Why you've been so damned scared of me all this time. You've idealized the past. As far as I know, no one's ever had a 'perfect' marriage. Don't you see? You've painted over the real memories with pretty pastel colors, so that nothing else will ever measure up. No man could possibly compete with your memories of Lon. Even Lon."

She stood abruptly, and the scarf came with her. One end of it trailed over the ground as she began to pace back and forth in front of him. "What is this, 'Pick on Gypsy Night'? What's the matter with you? Ever since you came back with the gas you've been in one foul mood."

"Yeah, you're right," he admitted. "But sometimes foul moods help me think more clearly. This one has, at any rate." When she turned away from him, he sighed. "Gypsy, hey. Don't do that, okay? I just want to talk."

"You didn't want to a few minutes ago."

"So? Can't I change my mind? Or is that still exclusively a woman's prerogative?"

She raised her eyes to the stars. "What you're doing, Keane, isn't talking, it's twisting. It's accusing. And I don't understand why."

"I'm not accusing, I'm just trying to tear down this block of yours."

"What *block*?"

He rose and went to her, turning her around in his arms. The feel of her, strong and warm against him, very nearly caused him to back down, but the constant reminder in his shirt pocket told him he couldn't. It was worse than a ticking clock, and this might be his last chance to break through her fear and make her see what she was doing to herself. Not to mention him. "Look," he said, "remember when I swore to you that this wasn't going to be a summer fling?"

Eyes wary, she nodded.

"Well, I meant it, and it hasn't been. At least, not for me. These past couple of days have been great. Hell, spectacular, why waste adjectives? But it's time we got to the point, Gypsy lady. We've got something special here, and we want it to go forward. Right or wrong?"

"Right," she whispered.

"Fine. So far, so good. But the thing is, if we do go forward, it's not always going to be fun and games. Sooner or later I'll do something that really ticks you off . . . well, more than usual, anyway. And you'll think to yourself, 'Omigod. He isn't what I expected him to be at all. He isn't Lon, and he'll never be Lon.' And then I'll be out on my ear."

"That's ridiculous!"

"Is it? For a while I thought, or hoped, that you were finally gearing up to make an emotional commitment again—"

"I am! Or at least, I'm trying." She fought her way out of his hold, and as she did the edge of her scarf caught on his belt buckle. Before either of them knew what was happening, the fragile silk tore down the middle and fluttered to the ground.

Gypsy simply stood and looked at it.

Keane put his hand over the buckle, as if that belated gesture could somehow make the scarf whole again. "I'm sorry."

"It's okay."

"No, it isn't. I'll buy you another one . . ."

"I said, it's okay."

"But—"

"Stop it!"

He closed his mouth and retreated, both hands raised.

Two or three minutes passed before she moved again. Then, with a slight shake of her head, she seemed to dismiss the incident. Up went that stubborn chin of hers he'd come to know so well, and there was a sparkle in her eye that had nothing to do with tears.

"Better this than napkins," she said.

"What?"

"You're wrong, you know."

What in heaven's name was she talking about? Keane cocked his head, totally confused. "Wrong?"

"About my comparing you to Lon. I'd never

throw you out on your ear because you weren't him."

He digested that, then, after one last glance at the ruined scarf, stepped forward. "You don't know how much I want to believe that," he said softly. "But I'm a realist, Gypsy. In my business you learn real fast that dreams aren't all they're cracked up to be. The world is always out there, and sooner or later it's bound to intrude. I know you'd like me to leave well enough alone, and when times are good it's easy to do that, to just let tomorrow take care of itself."

"Is that what you think I want? The easiest route?"

"Why not?" he asked. "It's less painful that way. But think about it. We're not going to be out here in the wide open spaces forever. Sooner than you think, maybe sooner than either of us is ready for, it's all going to change. There'll be more things standing in our way than clear skies and an empty field."

She stared at him, then very slowly sank down on the sleeping bag once more, her long legs folded beneath her. "You're trying to tell me your exile's over. They want you back, don't they?"

Keane hesitated before he removed the folded paper from his pocket. "That, uh, Roger kid didn't fly out here by accident today. He brought this, to give to me. I guess when he saw the Moth he got a little exuberant."

"What is it?"

"Telegram. From my editor in New York. 'Have had a helluva time tracking you down. Stop. Heat's off, so bring the fluff piece home. Stop. Another assignment awaits, Bitteman's orders.'" He closed his eyes and wadded the paper in his fist. "'Stop.'"

When Gypsy spoke next he could barely hear her. "So . . . what do we do now?"

"That's what I've been thinking about all evening. When I went to get the gas earlier I tried to call the offices. I had it in mind to wring another week out of Daniels, any way I could, but I forgot about the time difference back there. The upper echelon was gone for the day. It wouldn't have worked anyway."

"Why didn't you tell me before?"

He shrugged and sat down next to her. "I suppose I wanted to put it off as long as possible. I wanted to sort some things out in my head."

"And have you?"

Keane watched the way the lantern light glimmered through her hair, turning it to a deep burnished copper. Her eyes searched his and he tried to find the courage to hold them. All of a sudden he felt like a sixteen-year-old asking for a first date. "Gypsy, I can't just walk away from here and pretend we never happened. I've got to have some sense of the future, some sense of direction. I have to know . . ."

She said nothing when he paused, merely waited for him to continue.

He swallowed. "Meet me in Chicago in two weeks. That should give me enough time to wind up whatever I'm working on, and it's not far out of your way."

"Chicago?"

"Yes. It'll give us both a chance to think about

what we want to do from there. Say you will, Gypsy."

She folded her arms across her breasts in an unconsciously protective gesture. "I haven't wanted to speculate on what might happen when you were finished here."

"I know." Keane couldn't help but lean toward her, anxious now for an answer.

"I'm still scared," she whispered.

"I know that, too."

"I . . . saw a different side of you today, when you were so angry with that boy. Away from here, in the city, surrounded by thousands of people . . . you might become a stranger to me. And if for that reason it didn't work out . . . I'd almost rather we ended it here and now than to see it die like that."

Keane took her face in his hands and kissed her, very lightly. Afterward he didn't let her go. "Gypsy, love, look at me. I think you know me, really know me, better than anyone alive. If I lost my cool today it was because that kid endangered you. I'll admit, I could have taken his head off for that, but I didn't. I'm the same person. For better or worse, what you see is what you get. So please—meet me in Chicago."

Indecision flickered through her emerald eyes. Indecision and that same old fear. "Two weeks is a long time. Long enough for perspectives to change," she said, and her voice trembled a little. "All I can promise you is that I'll try. Don't push me any further than that, Keane."

The disappointment was strong. What had he expected, after all? A pledge of undying love and devotion? Keane tried not to let it show on his face, but one look at the guilt on hers told him he hadn't succeeded. He nodded curtly. "Fair enough. At least you didn't say no, so I guess there's still hope."

There didn't seem to be anything left to say, so he got up to retrieve his pencil and notebook from the Moth, then settled himself by the lantern.

"What are you doing?" Gypsy asked.

He lifted his head only briefly. "Gathering my notes. I have an article to write, and I'm not much in the mood for sleep. Don't let me keep you up, though." From the corner of his eye he saw how bereft she looked, sitting there, and he sensed her confusion. But there wasn't much he could do about it. She hadn't said no. Not directly. But why did he feel rejected, then? He shook his head as he realized that he had indeed expected unequivocal acceptance.

At last she moved, and he tried not to hear her preparing herself for bed, such as it was. Tried not to notice when she removed her jacket and boots, then stretched her arms high over her head, holding her body in an unknowingly sensuous arc. Everything about her was so natural and free—why couldn't her emotions be, as well?

In the air she was a dancer, with the Moth's wings for dancing shoes. On earth she remained a puzzle. Soon Keane's pencil began to track along the page, and after the first few halting lines, words came easy.

"Have you got your ticket?"
"Right here."
"Your camera case?"
"Mmm-hmm. It's already loaded."

Gypsy quickly scanned Ashford Grove's sparsely populated railway platform, as if she could spot something Keane may have forgotten. Gene and Linda stood close by, ready, she knew, to provide moral support if she needed it. *And I might*, she thought. *Before this is over, I just might.* "I called ahead. You'll be able to get a direct flight to New York City when you reach Rockford."

"Okay." Keane hefted his small travel bag and nodded. From behind them came the final boarding call. "I guess this is it, then." He turned to Gene and offered his hand. "Thanks for the taxi service."

"My pleasure. Glad to have met you. We'll be looking for that article."

"Right."

Linda glanced at Gypsy, then nudged her husband's arm. "Come on. Let's go wait for Gypsy in the car," she urged. "Maybe we'll see you again, Keane. Until then, take care."

"I hope so. Bye."

After they'd gone Gypsy slowly raised her eyes. Keane's were focused on her face, and whether he meant it to be or not, the question was still in them. He hadn't voiced it again, last night, or this morning, and she knew he wouldn't now either. It was, in every way, her move.

"What, no final word?" he asked, his voice a shade too jaunty. "I'm about to immortalize you, after all. The daring young woman in her flying machine. Next thing you know, your passengers will all want autographs as well as rides."

"I do appreciate what you'll be doing for Gallagher Aviation. I'm sure Neal will too."

"I didn't do it for Neal." He held her eyes for a

long moment, then looked down, adjusting his sport jacket.

"Keane . . ." she began.

"No. Don't say anything else." As though it required an enormous effort, he made himself look at her again. "For what it's worth, I'll never forget you, Erin Gallagher."

He started to turn away, thought better of it, then caught her roughly by the shoulders, kissing her with a forcefulness that startled her and caused her brain to whirl in a kaleidoscope of colors.

Before she got her breath back he was heading for the train.

She couldn't let it happen. All of a sudden it became a certainty. Even if she did end up losing him later, it couldn't feel any worse than losing him now.

The urgency rose within her, strong and sure, and as he reached the edge of the platform she called his name.

He halted but didn't look back.

"McCready!" she tried again, and this time he nearly knocked over another passenger as he faced her. "I'll do it!" she shouted.

"What?"

"I said, I'll do it! I'll come to Chicago!"

Several seconds passed; then he smiled and let out a whoop of joy.

The other travelers on the platform began to give him a wide berth.

"You'll come?" he asked, ignoring them.

Gypsy nodded. "Yes. I'll come!"

Swiftly he made his way back and hugged her, almost lifting her off her feet. "I'm not hearing things, am I?"

"No." She laughed. "Now get out of here before I change my mind."

"Right." He kissed her once more, then moaned when she made him break it off. "Two weeks from today. The Hilton."

"Got it."

"You're really coming?"

"How many times do I have to say it?"

"No more. I think I believe you. Hell, I think I love you!" With that, he turned on his heel and ran for the train, clapping an older man on the back as he passed him. "She's coming!" he proclaimed.

The man grinned and gave him a thumbs-up.

Gypsy watched him board, then stayed and watched as the train left the station. She didn't realize until she heard Linda calling her name that she was the last person on the platform.

"Gypsy, are you coming?"

She lifted her hand in a final wave at the departing train. "Now that the whole world knows it, I guess I'll have to."

"Huh?"

With a soft smile, Gypsy turned and joined her friend. "I'm coming. *I'm really coming.*"

CHAPTER
Six

"SHE'S NOT COMING." Keane leaned his forehead on the Hilton's cool windowpane and gazed out over Chicago's nighttime skyline. "It's seven forty-five. If she was coming, she'd be here by now. She must have changed her mind."

"Come on, Dad, you're just being paranoid," said a childish yet strangely wise voice behind him.

Keane turned and regarded his son with raised eyebrows. "Paranoid? Since when does an eight-year-old know a word like *paranoid*?"

"Since the school principal read one of your articles to us in assembly."

"Oh, really? Remind me to put in an appearance at your next PTA meeting." He moved away from the window and paced their suite, unable to remain still.

Kevin, a blond-haired, blue-eyed replica of Keane as a boy, sat smack in the center of one of the queen-sized beds, watching his father from behind wire-rimmed glasses. "I'm hungry," he pronounced. "Can we go have dinner now?"

"And what if she comes while we're in the restaurant? She wouldn't be able to find us."

"But I thought you said she wasn't coming."

"And I thought you said I was just being paranoid." Keane scrubbed his hands over his face. "Just fifteen more minutes, huh, Kev? Then we'll go." He adjusted his tie for the umpteenth time that evening, and involuntarily his mind drifted back over the past two weeks. It seemed more like two months.

Shortly after his arrival in New York he'd been dispatched to Southern California to cover a series of arson-caused brush fires in the area, but not before he'd met with Paul Daniels to discuss the Oshkosh/Gallagher piece.

Daniels, a tall, reed-thin man who wore his gray hair too long and his trousers too short, had perused Keane's material with an occasional quick nod, then frowned. "Not bad, not bad. Along the lines of what Bitteman's looking for, but—"

"But?" Keane sat on the edge of Daniels's desk, sifting through the myriad photographs he'd taken of the actual air show, and Gypsy. Gypsy stretched out against the Moth, backlit by that spectacular sunset; Gypsy in goggles and scarf, taken when he'd finally found the courage to turn all the way around in the front cockpit while in flight; Gypsy talking with the locals in Libertyville; Gypsy standing on top of the Moth; Gypsy standing beneath the Moth . . .

"From the tone of this article," Daniels told him, "Gypsy Gallagher seems more like some gossamer angel than a flesh-and-blood woman."

Keane, absorbed in a photo of Gypsy posing with the scarecrow, murmured, "Oh, she's a woman, all right."

"Confirmed it, have you?"

At the editor's tone, Keane slowly looked up.

"Oh, get that offended scowl off your face. This is me, remember? What you did or didn't do with her is your own affair, so to speak. I really don't care one way or the other. But as far as the article is concerned, we're going to need a little more meat, Keane. You're overestimating your audience here. They don't want to read about some lighter-than-air goddess who's a cross between Rita Hayworth and Mother Teresa. We've got to give her more dimension."

Keane made a grab for his typewritten pages, but Daniels pulled them out of his reach. "What do you mean, 'we,' bwana?"

Daniels sighed as he leaned back in his chair. "Keane, Keane. I'm not going to rewrite your piece, okay? I'm talking about adding a sidebar, maybe. A little additional background info you were probably too . . . preoccupied to dig up."

"Such as?"

"Such as the accident that killed her husband. See, the name 'Gallagher' rang a bell to me after you called that day, so I did a little checking in the newspaper morgues. It was a fairly big story at the time. Seems there was even some talk of pilot error or mechanical negligence. Rumors, mind you, but interesting rumors."

Keane felt the blood drain from his face, then just as quickly return. "So, *World View* prints rumors now," he said, voice deadly soft.

"Rumors are an inescapable part of life."

When at last he understood that the man wasn't kidding, Keane stood and began to gather his photographs.

"Hey," Daniels objected. "I'm going to need those."

"No, you're not. And you won't need my copy, either." This time when he reached for the pages, he got them.

"Keane, for God's sake, what are you doing? Quitting again? Sorry, you're rehired. I could go head to head with you over this all day, but you have a plane to catch, remember?"

Later, Keane could barely recall what he said next. Something about integrity and humanity. Then a speech that included everything from friendship to corporate values. He concluded with, "Paul, I swear it, if you print a word of that tripe under my byline, I'm out of *World View*. I'll go down the block to *Time* and give them an exposé they'd kill for."

Daniels had stared at him, accustomed to his frequent outbursts, yet shocked by his newest threat. In the end he relented, and Keane had reluctantly given the article and photos back to him. In a potato field in Wisconsin Gypsy had come to trust him, and he intended to keep that trust. Because in two weeks she was coming to Chicago . . .

"She's not coming," he groaned as he continued to pace the hotel suite. It was now eight P.M. Past Kevin's dinnertime, and past hope. Something must have caused her to change her mind. Something he'd said or done at the last moment. Or maybe her insecurities had surfaced after he left. Maybe her friends had talked her out of it.

"Dad . . ."

"Huh?"

"Dinner?"

"Oh. Yeah." Keane ran a hand through his hair, then smoothed it self-consciously. What if they met her on the way to the lobby? Could be she was only delayed. Bad weather, perhaps. Or engine trouble. Now why did he have to go and think a thing like that? He'd call O'Hare right away, see if she filed a flight plan. "Is my tie straight?" he asked Kevin.

The boy rolled his eyes heavenward. "Man, are you paranoid."

Nothing like a little bad luck to bring out the paranoia, thought Gypsy with a grimace.

The country music blaring from the jukebox behind her only made her headache worse. Leaning her elbows on the bar of the Final Approach coffee shop, located on a general aviation airstrip just outside Ottawa, Illinois, she massaged her tired eyes.

It was past eight. Keane must have given up on her by now. How long would he wait before assuming she'd gotten another attack of the relationship jitters and chickened out?

"Looks like you need something a little stronger than a cup of tea."

She glanced up. A lean, angular woman, around forty-five, with graying blond hair and a ready smile, had settled herself two stools down. Not in the mood for chitchat, Gypsy muttered, "Gas. I need gas."

"Oh, yeah? Some of Donald's chili ought to fix you up right, then." She laughed, and when Gypsy didn't follow suit, just as soon sobered. "It was only a joke, honey. Look, if you want me to shut up and mind my own business, say so. Plenty of other people have, and it hasn't clipped my wings yet."

At that, Gypsy couldn't help but smile. "I'm sorry. I'm just . . . wrapped up in my own problems."

"One look around here tells me you're not the only bird grounded. The name's Billie, by the way. No last name, just Billie." She extended a raw-boned hand.

Gypsy took it and found it surprisingly warm. "Gypsy Gallagher. They tell me the gas truck won't be here till morning."

"That's a fact. In the meantime, all these tanks are dry as dust. Where you headed?"

"Chicago. I should have been there hours ago; I have to meet someone."

"Business?"

Gypsy hesitated, but something in the woman's eyes beckoned her to spill all. What could it hurt? she reasoned. A friendly ear might be exactly what she needed right now. After a deep breath, she began. "It all started in Oshkosh . . ."

"It all started in Oshkosh, see?" Keane told their polite but increasingly impatient waiter. "I met this—"

"Dad, come on."

Kevin nudged his arm and he turned. "What?"

"He only asked if we want dessert."

Keane shook his head and glanced around the elegant dining room as if for the first time. All of a sudden he felt out of place, confined. It was only a ritual. Sit down, order food, talk softly till it arrived, eat; then tip the waiter for his role in the practiced craft of dining out. Why hadn't he ever been able to see through it before now? He folded his cloth napkin beside his half-eaten meal. "I don't want anything else, thanks. You order whatever you want, Kev; I'll be right back."

"Where you going?"

"To get some air."

He wandered aimlessly out into the hotel's lobby, and felt guilty for bringing his son along on this ill-fated trip. He'd promised Kevin an outing, and what had he delivered? A day and half a night cooped up in a hotel room, in a city he'd already visited at least three or four times in his young life. Chicago wasn't the place to bring an eight-year-old boy. Chicago was a rendezvous for lovers, a trysting spot on the road to domestic bliss. A place that, when you were both old and gray, you could come back to, and relive those wild, romantic times of youth.

Oh, come off it, McCready, he told himself. You're not that young, you never were terribly romantic, and the woman you fell in love with out there in the fields doesn't exist. You made her up, sport. All those times you thought you were flying? Hallucinations. Daniels was right, a woman like that couldn't be real. Real women honored promises, didn't they?

There weren't any phone calls left to make. O'Hare had no record of any flight plan filed in her name. No freak storms had sprung up near here. He stopped near the entrance and looked out at the glittering night. "Gypsy, where the hell are you? What are you *doing*?"

"What am I doing?" Gypsy groaned over her fifth cup of tea. "I shouldn't be boring you to death with all this."

Billie's eyes widened, as did her ever-present smile. "Honey, you have got to be kidding. What you've just told me is...beautiful. It's inspiring. It's...hell, it's better than one of those romance novels Del sells me down at the used-book store."

Gypsy ran her hands through her hair and gave the older woman a wan smile in return.

"It's also, if you want my opinion, too good to give up on."

"I tried calling his hotel in Chicago." She sighed. "It seems the only phone in this place has been out of order for the past three days."

"Oh, my..." Billie stood and shouted to the man behind the counter. "Donald, doesn't anything work around here anymore? You ought to be ashamed."

The man spread his hands and shrugged.

"Really, Billie, it's all right," Gypsy assured her.

"No, it isn't all right." She lowered her voice as she turned away from the counter. "Come outside with me."

"What?"

"Don't you argue, I said come outside."

Confused, Gypsy did as she was told and followed her out into the warm night air.

Once she was sure no one could overhear them, Billie dropped her bombshell. "I'm taking you to Chicago myself, girl."

Gypsy's heartbeat quickened. "But how...?"

"I just happen to have me a little Cessna one fifty-two parked a couple of hangars down. Fuel tank's full. How much you weigh, hon?"

"Uh, one twenty-five or so."

"Perfect, we'll still be underweight, provided

you're not carrying two-ton luggage. Are you with me?"

"What about my biplane?"

"You can use my tie-down for tonight, and I'll get you another one tomorrow. When you come back, she'll be all gassed up and waiting for you. Come on, girl, I'm on a roll, you can't turn me down now. You said yourself, if you wait till the morning it'll most likely be too late."

Gypsy chewed her lip as she watched the other woman and considered her words. Hope had begun to take the place of the emptiness inside her. Would Keane wait? She had no way of knowing, but she'd be a fool to take the chance and pass this opportunity by. She took a deep breath and pushed the night out of stall. "You're on."

Fifteen minutes later she wondered if she'd have cause to regret her decision. The tiny Cessna, though only a few years old, was a near-wreck.

"My God, how could you let an airplane get into such a condition?" she asked as she climbed into the right seat.

"Don't you worry," Billie told her. "She may be sagging on the outside, but she's raring to go on the inside. Takes after me." After a standard preflight check she pushed the starter button and the single-engine plane coughed into feeble life.

Gypsy closed her eyes. "Just answer me one question. How do you keep this thing in the air, much less fly her?"

"The same way I do everything else." Her benefactress laughed as they began to taxi down the deserted runway. "On a wing and a prayer!"

If I live through this, Gypsy thought, you'd better be waiting for me, Keane McCready.

"Thirty minutes. I'll wait another thirty minutes, but that's it," Keane muttered, straightening his tie in the mirror behind the bar where he slowly nursed a watered-down scotch.

After Kevin had finished his dessert, he'd taken him on up to the suite and tucked him safely into bed, then returned to the ground floor of the hotel and found a lounge close to the entrance. If by some wild quirk of fate Gypsy happened to walk through that door, he'd be johnny-on-the-spot. That's what he told himself, anyway. Maybe he really had an incipient desire to play the jilted lover, the righteously indignant hero, down on his luck and well into his cups. Somehow, he knew, the role didn't quite suit him. He'd never been the cry-in-his-beer type.

Funny. He'd wanted so much for Gypsy to meet Kevin, and vice versa. Kevin was a little introverted, and he knew Gypsy was good with kids. He'd seen it time and time again out in the fields. She'd make a hell of a mother one day, if she allowed herself to get that far.

He ran an impatient hand through his hair, smoothed it, then took another sip of his drink. Maybe if I hadn't said "I love you," he reasoned. A line guaranteed to scare off even the most stalwart of the human race.

Keane had a feeling he was in the process of finding out why.

"Right about here is where Charlie bailed out,"

Billie shouted over the whine of the Cessna's engine. "Just west of Marseilles."

I don't blame him, Gypsy wanted to say, but held her tongue. The lights of tiny Marseilles, still approximately sixty miles from Chicago, twinkled beneath them, and the air, warmed by the heat of the late-summer day, was bumpy and unpredictable. Except for that small reminder of civilization, the world outside was pitch dark, and they flew on instruments alone. Which, of course, made it impossible to pinpoint any level stretches of ground should an emergency landing be necessary. The first rule of flight, her father had taught her long ago, was to be on constant lookout for a place to set down. Shaking her head, she made herself ask, "Who's Charlie?"

"Why, Charlie Lindbergh, of course. Nineteen twenty-six, it was, before he took on the Atlantic. He was flying the mail route from St. Louis to Chicago, in a deHavilland, if I remember what my daddy told me. Hit some fog and couldn't land, so he decided to backtrack by his compass and parachute out over what he hoped was an unpopulated area. His plane landed about three hundred yards from our farm, and he came down nary a mile away. It was the talk of the town that year, I'll tell you."

"Really?" was all Gypsy could manage as they hit a particularly nasty air pocket. Though she'd been through worse herself, many times, somehow it was different when she wasn't at the controls. Now she was able to sympathize with some of the things Keane must have felt on his first few flights with her. Thank God it wasn't foggy out, at least.

She tried to relax and thought instead about the

past two weeks. About the anticipation that had grown stronger with each day. The sky, her beloved escape hatch from the world, no longer seemed as inviting, and the Moth felt empty without the man she'd grown accustomed to seeing in the front cockpit. With an ache that was almost physical she found she missed their conversations beneath the wing, their frequent arguments, and most of all, the feel of his body, warm and vital beside her at night.

Several times she'd damned him for turning the aloneness she'd always cherished into an enemy. Then, just as quickly, she'd regret it and wish his arms were around her.

At the beginning of the second week she called Neal and told him about the article Keane planned, and her reasons for granting the interview in the first place. To her surprise, he was all for it. Only when she explained her own hesitation because of Lon's accident did he grow testy.

"Do you have reason to mistrust the man still?" he asked her.

"Of course not, not now. What happened at Oshkosh was partly misunderstanding and partly my own overreaction."

"Realize that, do you?"

"In hindsight, yes." It was then that she found the courage to broach a subject both of them had avoided for too many years. "Neal, I've never asked you this before, maybe because I was afraid of what you'd tell me. The night before Lon died, you were with him in the Pilot's Pub. How did he . . . seem to you?"

For a while she thought they'd lost the long-distance connection, the line was so silent. When he spoke again, his voice sounded strange. "I don't reckon this is somethin' we ought to discuss over the telephone, darlin'. Best wait till you get home."

"No, it's got to be now. I won't go into why, but it's very important that I know. It's...time. Please?"

She spent a frustrating few minutes trying to convince him, but in the end he relented, though it was obvious the words came hard.

"Lon told me about the fight the two of you had earlier that evening," he said softly.

Gypsy held her breath. "And?"

"And, he was a mite upset by it."

"How upset?"

"Gypsy, girl..."

"Please, Neal."

He sighed into the receiver. "Upset enough to tip a few more than he was used to. I warned him to ease off, but he'd got his Irish up..."

Gypsy hadn't heard any more. Closing her eyes, she whispered, "Oh, my God. Then it might have been true after all."

The lights of Marseilles faded behind the Cessna as she and Billie neared their destination. She hadn't realized it till now, but her nails were digging into her palms.

Keane had to be there. There was so much she needed to tell him.

Well, her thirty minutes were up. Actually, he'd given her the benefit of the doubt and allowed her forty-five.

Keane paid up his tab and left the lounge, then checked the front desk for any messages. None.

How could she blithely assume he had all this time to waste? He was a busy man, after all. It had taken some juggling for him to clear these three days, and one of them was already gone. Instead of waiting for Gypsy Gallagher, he could have taken Kevin to the park today, or even the zoo. Instead of wasting time right now he could be upstairs, doing some serious . . . sleeping.

A sudden commotion in the lobby behind him almost made him turn, but he decided he'd rather not risk the disappointment and headed in the opposite direction of the hubbub, toward the elevators.

You've got to stop imagining every sound you hear is her, he told himself sternly. You've got to stop expecting her to call out from across the crowded room—

"Keane!"

He froze in midstride, causing a bellhop with a dolly full of luggage to make a sharp left around him.

"Keane, wait!"

There it was again. Either the scotch had been stronger than he thought, or that voice belonged to a very familiar person. He forced himself to turn and willed it not to be a dream.

Gypsy struggled past the obstinate doorman, and into the lobby of the Hilton. A crowd began to gather around her after she spotted Keane near the elevators.

It didn't matter to her that she wasn't exactly dressed for the luxurious hotel. There hadn't been time enough to change once she and Billie finally touched down at O'Hare, and a chance encounter with a filthy mud-and-grease puddle outside a Yellow Cab had decorated her jeans, and probably her face, with a sooty finishing touch. All that mattered now was that she get to Keane before someone managed to throw her out of the place.

"Keane, wait!" she called again in desperation, and at last he turned and saw her.

His eyes widened and a slow grin spread across his face before he realized she was being detained; then he sobered fast and hurried to the edge of the crowd.

"What the hell's going on?" he asked the doorman, who had managed to grab Gypsy's arm once more.

"He won't let me through!"

The desk clerk, alerted to the fracas, hurried out from behind his post and confronted Keane. "Sir. Do you know this woman?"

"You're damned right I know this woman! The suite next to mine is reserved in her name."

"And that name is?"

Keane stared. "I don't believe this. Gallagher, all right?"

"One moment."

They all waited in suspended silence while the clerk went to check his computer. In less than a minute he was back, red-faced.

"Well?" Keane asked.

"I'm terribly sorry, Mr. McCready, for the misunderstanding. Of course Ms. Gallagher is welcome." He turned to the startled doorman. "Let her go, Rudy."

Gypsy stepped back when he released her arm.

With as much dignity as she could muster, she hefted her single suitcase and waded through the gawking crowd toward Keane. He held her eyes as she approached, and by the time she stopped before him it was as though they were the only two people in the room.

She pushed back a muddy strand of hair from her cheek and smiled. "Bet you gave up on me, didn't you?"

A peculiar expression crossed his features and he patted the lapel of his immaculate dark suit. "Me, give up? Don't be ridiculous. I knew you'd come."

In the next instant, heedless of his jacket, he was squeezing the life out of her.

Gypsy closed her eyes and reveled in the familiar musky scent of his cologne. "Sure you did, McCready," she whispered next to his ear. "But I know when you're lying. Something to do with body language . . ."

CHAPTER
Seven

GYPSY FELT A LITTLE like Dorothy entering the
Emerald City when she opened the door to her
suite. It was gorgeous, all done up in shades of blue
and beige. There were even fresh flowers in crystal
vases, and a bottle of champagne rested in a bath of
melted ice atop a silver cart.

Slowly she took a step forward. "So, this is how
the other half lives, huh?"

Keane chuckled beside her. "Nothing's too good
for you. Or for Kevin. I figured I might as well go
all the way and do this thing right."

"Kevin?"

"Oh, yeah, didn't I mention? I brought him
along with me. Incidentally, that's the only reason
I'm not ushering you into my own suite right now."
He frowned suddenly at her silence. "You don't
mind, do you? It's just that I've been promising him
we'd spend some time together, and . . ." He broke
off. "What? Why are you looking at me that way?"

"Because it was a wonderful idea, you nitwit, and
don't you dare apologize. I'd love to meet him."

He smiled with relief and put her suitcase on the
plush blue sofa. "And he's dying to meet you. I

118

hope you're prepared to live up to all the tall tales I've been telling him."

"Tall tales?"

"Figure of speech." He let his eyes roam over her from head to toe. "Oh, Gypsy, am I glad to see you. You're . . . you're absolutely scuddy; what happened?"

"Let's just say we both owe Billie a happy ending."

"Who's—?"

She silenced him with the palm of her hand, then with a kiss. "Later. I'll tell you all about it later. But first you can point me in the general direction of the bathroom so I can take a nice, civilized hot shower and change."

His arms snaked around her and tightened. "Need somebody to scrub your back? Or anything else, for that matter?"

"Mmm, sounds tempting, but I think I can manage."

"Oh, drat." He buried his face in her shoulder. "You're no fun at all, Miss Gallagher."

Gypsy smiled, disengaged herself, and retrieved her case from the sofa. "Ms., didn't you hear the desk clerk? Now, which way is the tub?"

He pointed toward the bedroom.

"Thanks. Oh, and so there's no misunderstanding—I'm paying for my own rooms, Keane."

"Oh, come on," he said after a pause. "I invited you, it's my treat. Besides, these prices are astronomical, and—"

She lifted her chin a fraction. "And?"

Seeing that retreat was the better part of valor, at least for the moment, he raised a hand and nodded.

"And... don't wash yourself down the drain, my Gypsy lady. I'm going over to check on Kevin, and I want you out here and ready to party in twenty-five minutes, you got me?"

"Twenty-five? Why not thirty?"

"Humor me, okay? My male ego forces me to act like the boss in some areas, so it's thirty... I mean, twenty-five. Hell, just hurry, please?"

He looked so little-boy vulnerable standing there, it was all Gypsy could do not to rush back to him that instant. "Well, since you put it that way, I'll try my best to make it twenty," she promised.

Keane softly closed the connecting door between his and Gypsy's suites, then checked his watch. Five minutes to spare.

The water had stopped and he could hear her humming to herself in the bathroom. Rubbing his hands together, he crossed to the champagne cart, unable to subdue a wide grin. She was here, she was—more or less—his, and for all intents and purposes, all was now right with his world.

The grin soon faded. Ice. While he'd been downstairs in the lounge the ice had melted, and the champagne was only semicold. Damn!

Three minutes left. Keane rushed to the phone and punched the number for room service, ordered more ice, then on second thought, another vase of fresh flowers. It couldn't hurt, and besides, he was billing everything to his expense account for *World View*. Daniels owed him that much, and more.

With a minute and a half to liftoff, he settled back on the sofa. The fact that she'd come must mean she had every intention of prolonging their

relationship. Whatever difficulties she'd had to sur-
mount to get to him only reinforced that, didn't it?
While he and Kevin had been enjoying dinner, lord
only knew where she—

"Oh, no."

Dinner. She probably hadn't had a chance to eat.
She must be starved, but knowing her she wouldn't
mention it.

Back to the phone. "Hello, room service? This is
suite one-oh-one-two again. I also need . . ." My
God, besides beef stew, what did the woman like?
Think, McCready. When the two of you went out to
dinner in Libertyville, what did she have? For the
life of him, he couldn't remember. "Uh, yes, I'm
still here. Dammit, why can't I remember? No, I'm
not talking to you, I just—"

The bathroom doorknob began to turn.

"Strawberries and cream!" he whispered ur-
gently. "Yeah, that's it. Strawberries and cream.
Yeah, thanks. And if you get it here in the next ten
minutes I'll double the tip. Um-hm, right."

The door opened as he replaced the receiver.
"Who were you calling?" she asked.

Keane cleared his throat. "The time. Just making
sure you came in under the limit." When he looked
up at her all the blood seemed to rush from his head
and he placed an unsteady hand on the arm of the
sofa.

She was his Gypsy, yet she wasn't. She wore a
very light, very chic silk dress the color of peach,
with thin spaghetti straps and a layered, uneven
hem that reached as low as her calves and as high as
midthigh. She'd brushed her hair to a brilliant auburn sheen, and her skin, so flawless without

makeup, looked all the more lovely with it. The faint scent of her perfume wafted its way to him and he could only stand in mesmerized silence. She'd entered the hotel a free-spirited, leather-and-jeans-clad individualist—albeit a wildly sexy one—and managed in less than half an hour to transform herself into the kind of elegant woman a *Vogue* cover girl would envy.

She smiled a little self-consciously at his reaction. "Linda and I went shopping before I left Ashford Grove." When he simply continued to stare, she stepped forward. "Is Kevin all right?"

Keane had to force his voice to respond. "He's, uh ... fine. Sound asleep."

"Then I guess I'll have to wait till morning to meet him."

"His loss, my gain." He closed the distance between them and touched her, half expecting her to vanish like some desert mirage. But the feel of her soft bare skin beneath his palms was real enough, and when her breath caught at the contact, he groaned, pulling her close against him. "God, but I missed you."

"Every day?"

"Every day, every hour, every second."

"And I thought *I* was crazy."

He sought and found her lips, unable to hold back the rush of overwhelming emotion. Her response was pure fire, and soon her hands were climbing up inside his jacket, moving over his body, the only obstacle his thin shirt. Keane didn't want any obstacles at all. None of the trappings meant anything now. Not the sumptuous surroundings, not the champagne, not the silk dress she'd obviously spent a small fortune on to please him.

Slowly he lowered her to the floor, and in his imagination the carpet became grass, and the air conditioning a soft southerly breeze. The past magic came over both of them once again as they began to undress one another. Only this time the urgency of their first encounter seemed pale in comparison. His shirt buttons flew in all directions at the insistence of her impatient hands and, without knowing quite how he did it, he managed to remove her dress and send it sailing across the room to land in a puddle of silk before the door.

"Does that mean you didn't like it?" she asked on an unsteady breath.

"I love it. But I love you more."

She hadn't bothered with the encumbrance of a bra. Keane closed his eyes and tasted the tender flesh of her nipples, still redolent of soap, then groaned as she arched upward. When what remained of their clothing lay strewn in a haphazard ring around them, he gathered enough of his wits together to ask, "Do you love me, Gypsy? If you do, I want to hear you say it."

Her eyelids fluttered open in surprise.

"Say it," he repeated, too far gone to worry about pushing her now. He had needs, too, and one of them was to hear the words she'd said over and over to him in his dreams, but never in reality. Dreams could come true; tonight was proof. He lowered his mouth to her throat and traced a moist path down her skin with the very tip of his tongue.

She shuddered.

"Say it, Gypsy lady." He wasn't sure she heard

him that time, because it came out in a bare whisper. But soon her hands were on either side of his head, pulling him up to face her directly.

Her eyes sparkled with a hint of unshed tears, and she had to swallow a couple of times to get the words out. But they came, nonetheless. "I love you, Keane McCready."

He surrendered himself into her keeping then, certain he'd never be happier than he was at that moment.

A muted knock came at the door before they'd quite managed to regain their breath.

"Who could that be?" Gypsy asked him.

At first he had no idea, then full memory came flooding back. "Oh, no, it's the stuff I ordered from room service."

"What 'stuff'?"

The knock came again, yet he made no move to get up. "Ice, strawberries, flowers, things like that."

She smiled, a lazy, sensuous smile that promised even more wonderful things. "Do we really need them?"

"Where we're going, I seriously doubt it."

"Oh, and where might that be?"

He stood suddenly and drew her up after him, then lifted her in his arms. "The bedroom, you fool for love. As long as we're here, we may as well find out what a proper mattress feels like, wouldn't you say?"

"What about that poor man out there with a cart full of strawberries and flowers?"

"Let him get his own girl."

* * *

The hotel coffee shop wasn't yet crowded when Gypsy entered early the next morning, so she had her pick of tables. Feeling a bit claustrophobic, she chose one near the window, and marveled again at the hustle and bustle of city life just outside. Though she hadn't been away from that life for very long herself, it seemed as though a great deal of time had passed since she left Oshkosh. A lot of water under the proverbial bridge.

"Here, let me," said her escort as he held a chair for her.

"Why, thank you, sir."

"You're welcome, Miss Gallagher."

"Call me Gypsy." She turned her coffee cup right side up without delay.

He followed her example and did the same.

"Do you think he knows we're down here?" she asked.

"If he did, he would've followed us. But he didn't, so that means he's still asleep."

She nodded, thoughtful. "Just the same, I feel a little guilty."

"It'll be okay. Trust me."

A waitress caught their eye and hurried over with a steaming pot of coffee.

Gypsy looked at her partner's cup. "I'll admit, it was very kind of you to invite me out like this, but shouldn't you be ordering milk . . . or something?"

He blinked behind thick lenses. "How about we compromise, and I get orange juice?"

For a moment she was speechless. "That sounded exactly like something your father would say. Are you sure you're only eight?"

After they ordered the juice, Kevin McCready

shrugged self-consciously. "I have a genius IQ. Or at least that's what my teachers keep telling Mom. But don't let my dad know, okay?"

"Why on earth not? I know he'd be very proud."

"Yeah, maybe. But he might think I don't need him . . . you know, to teach me things. I wouldn't want him to feel like that."

Gypsy took a welcomed sip of coffee and studied him. Though his words were insightful, containing more than a modicum of maturity, his eyes were childishly earnest, and she sensed that in reality it was the other way around. The son was afraid he'd alienate the father. A strange breed, these McCready men.

In the wee hours of the morning an exhausted Keane had stumbled from her suite to his own through the connecting door. He didn't want Kevin waking up alone, only to discover that his father's bed hadn't been slept in. But somehow the boy had suspected Gypsy's arrival, and when she emerged in search of caffeine a short time ago, she found him waiting for her in the hall. They'd recognized one another immediately, and hit it off even faster.

Now she grasped his hand across the table. "I'll tell you what. I'll promise to keep your secret, if you promise to keep mine. Deal?"

She could almost see his thought processes at work—wondering if she was worthy of his trust, deciding he really didn't have much choice, then reaching a final conclusion. "Deal," he said several seconds later. "But what kind of a secret could you have?"

"That I almost changed my mind about coming here to meet your dad. I didn't know what to expect, and I let my imagination run wild. Then I realized something very important. Something I'd been hiding from myself for a long time. And I knew that I owed it to him, and to me, to try to make it." Gypsy shook her head. Here she was, confiding in an eight-year-old as though he were Sigmund Freud. Yet she sensed a peculiar understanding behind that innocent face and those owlish, sky-blue eyes.

"Are you glad you came, then?" he asked her.

She remembered the reunion she and Keane shared the night before and wondered if the boy could read the sparkle in her own eyes. "Yes, I'm glad."

"You like my dad a lot, don't you?"

She couldn't suppress a wide smile. "You got me there. I confess."

"Good, 'cause he was a basket case before you showed up. Maybe now he'll settle down and we can have some fun. He told me we'd go see the—"

"Basket case?" Gypsy leaned forward. "I think you and I have some serious talking to do, Kevin. Tell me everything and I'll buy you a stack of pancakes a mile high, smothered in maple syrup."

The youthful enthusiasm she'd known was there surfaced at last, and he grinned, revealing a missing bottom tooth. "All *right*!"

"You'll spill all, then?"

"Everybody's got their price," he reasoned. "Well, everybody except Captain Commando, that is."

"Are you certain you were born, and not cloned?" she asked as she signaled the waitress.

* * *

Later that day, after Keane had dragged himself out of bed, the three of them explored the zoological garden and the bird sanctuary in Lincoln Park. Then, after a light lunch, Keane took them shopping at Marshall Field's.

While Kevin, entranced, watched a computer demonstration, the elder McCready dragged Gypsy to the ladies' department.

"Oh, no, you are absolutely not going to buy me anything," she said firmly as they passed through lingerie. "Especially not any of this. What would your son think?"

"Nothing he probably doesn't already know." He winked. "Don't worry, I'm not going to buy you a see-through negligee, or a lacy teddy, however fetching you might look in one. I much prefer you in nothing at all."

"Then where are we going?"

"I have a debt to pay, my lady of the skies. And I mean to do it, right now."

He pulled her through a crowd of women gathered around a sale table, and they emerged in millinery, facing a display case filled with multicolored scarves.

"No arguments," he told her when she opened her mouth to protest.

It took him nearly half an hour to convince the salesgirl he wanted simple white silk, and not mauve or fuchsia, but in the end he came away satisfied, and proudly draped his gift around Gypsy's neck.

This time it was he who reminded her of Kevin, and of the look on the boy's face as he dug into his pancakes that very morning. Something to do with the dimples. That look, as much as the beautiful scarf he'd bestowed, brought tears to her eyes. "Well, what do you think?" she asked him through the solid lump in her throat. "Am I dashing again?"

"I'd say Snoopy has some real competition."

As at the hotel, their surroundings seemed to fade, and she couldn't have cared less if the entire store was watching. She drew him close and gave him the longest, most passionate kiss he'd probably ever received.

When they parted at last, he stared at her, and soon the dimple reappeared. "Let's go find Kev and get outta here."

After a late dinner they packed a sleepy Kevin off to bed, then walked across Lake Shore Drive to Grant Park. Buckingham Fountains, near the center, sparkled upward into the night sky, a wonder of prismatic colors. They took their time strolling around them, and Gypsy felt a contentment she'd never before experienced on the ground. Since the evening was warm she wore the peach dress again, with the newly purchased scarf draped loosely over her shoulders. Keane's hand was cool and smooth against the bare flesh of her arm.

"Beautiful city," she remarked.

"Mmm." He pulled his eyes away from her and glanced at the fairyland of cascading water. "Thanks for letting me show it to you. Of course, it's not nearly as beautiful as what you've shown me from the cockpit of that Moth of yours. Are you sure it's safe in . . . Where did you say you left it?"

"In Ottawa. And yes, I trust Billie to take good care of her for me."

"This Billie sounds like quite a character."

Gypsy smiled. "She is. But an endearing one."

"Tell me something." Keane stopped to face her, and the lights from the fountain backlit him with a glowing aura. "Am I the only person you haven't gotten along with at first meeting?"

"One of the few," she acknowledged.

"Interesting. So . . . what did you and Kevin talk about at breakfast?"

"Oh . . . secrets."

"Secrets." He nodded. "Why does that make me feel distinctly suspicious?"

"I have no idea. Maybe you're just paranoid."

His eyes narrowed at that and he cleared his throat. "Uh-huh. I see I'm going to have to teach that son of mine a thing or two about confidential sources."

"Don't worry yourself, I won't hold it against you. As a matter of fact, I kind of liked seeing you through Kevin's eyes. He showed me a whole new side of you—vulnerable instead of obnoxious, eager to please, as opposed to—"

"All right, already, I get the message. All kidding aside, though, I *was* a wreck last night. I managed to convince myself at least a dozen times, and for a dozen different reasons, that you didn't want to see me again. That I'd done or said something that, in retrospect, caused you to have second thoughts about us."

"And now?"

"Now. . . ." He laughed softly. "Now I'm afraid to pinch myself in case this is a dream. I guess I'm still paranoid, huh?"

"I guess. I'm sorry I gave you reason to be, Keane; I didn't mean to."

"I know."

"You charged into my life like a bull through a china shop, and it took me by complete surprise."

"I'm sorry."

"No, don't be. That's what it took to get my attention, apparently. You were a mirror of sorts, and every time I looked at you, I saw what was wrong in me. So I lashed out. It took me a while to see that there were good things, too."

"It sounds like you've given this a lot of thought." His arm came around her and they began to walk once more.

Gypsy took a deep breath. This was the perfect opportunity to tell him. "Keane, there's something I—"

He shushed her with a hand to her lips. "Let's not risk spoiling the evening with any more talk, huh? Call me paranoid if you want, but every time we start to delve, I come close to losing you. I just got you back again, and I want the dream to go on a while longer."

"But I—"

"Just for tonight, okay?" He pulled one end of her scarf around his own neck, then tied both ends together. "Bonds of love." He smiled. "We'll talk tomorrow, all right? I swear, first thing."

"Tomorrow," she agreed softly, and they both shifted their eyes to the fountains.

Their promised talk seemed to be more elusive than she'd suspected. Keane's itinerary kept them hopping till noon the next day, and by the time they got back to the hotel for lunch and a change of clothes, all Gypsy could think of was a cool drink and a long leisurely soak in her suite's oversized bathtub.

If she didn't know him better she would have sworn Keane was overloading their schedule on purpose, perhaps to avoid getting down to the nitty gritty. But, like their barnstorming idyll, this trip had to come to an end sometime. Practicalities would have to be dealt with. They each had separate lives waiting for them, in separate states. He might be content for the moment to let their future dangle, yet now that she'd made this final leap toward commitment his attitude troubled her. Somewhere en route between Ashford Grove and Chicago they'd reversed roles. The shoe was on the other foot, and Gypsy found it an extremely tight fit.

They were passing the gift shop in the lobby when a page began to chant a few feet away. "Keane McCready. Telephone call for Keane McCready..."

He threw Gypsy a quizzical look, then moved forward and touched the young woman's arm. "I'm McCready."

"Yes, sir. You can take your call right over there." She pointed to a hotel phone near the check-in desk.

"Who'd be calling me here?" he wondered aloud after thanking her.

"You'll never find out if you don't answer," Gypsy said.

"Right. You and Kev go on ahead. Oh, and call

room service while you're at it. Order anything you want, just make it a lot—I'm starved."

"Gotcha." As Keane headed for the phone she turned to Kevin. "Well, I guess it's you and me, kid. Let's go."

"Wait a minute. This gift shop has a comics rack I should check out."

He pulled her toward the entrance, but she hung back. "Oh, Kevin, can't you do that later? I'm wrung out."

"You go up, then. I'll stay here and wait on Dad."

"And shirk my responsibilities? Not on your life. You know and I know you're not going to get lost, but your dad doesn't, remember."

"Then come on." He grasped her hand again. "It'll only take a minute."

"Why can't I ever say no to you guys?"

Once inside, Gypsy busied herself looking at curios. One item, a mobile with tiny silver biplanes, she decided she had to buy for Keane, no matter the cost. After she paid for it she joined Kevin at the door. "See what you made me do, you little urchin? What did you find?"

He pulled a couple of comics and a magazine from his bag. "*Troglodytes*, number eighteen, and *G.I. Men*, number fifty-nine. Oh, and I got this for you. The new *World View*. Dad's article about you is in it."

Slowly Gypsy took it from him. Sure enough, a colorful shot of the Oshkosh convention graced its slick cover, along with a small inset photo of herself. "He, uh . . . didn't tell me it'd be out this soon," she murmured.

"I've been watching for it. He told me he corrected the galley proofs last week."

"Galley proofs?"

"Yeah. That's the final edit of the article before it goes into print."

She nodded dumbly. "Well . . . let's get upstairs so I can read it, shall we, smart guy?"

In the privacy of her suite's bathroom she turned with shaking fingers to the page number listed in the contents. She didn't want Keane to interrupt her before she'd read the entire story. To have him watching her every reaction would be unnerving, to say the least.

In actuality, there were two articles. The first was on Oshkosh in general, and the second, adjacent story, focused solely on her. The photo on the facing page must have been one of those he'd taken that first evening, in the glow of the setting sun as she waited him out by the Moth. She smiled when she remembered how angry she'd been afterwards.

Above Keane's byline was the title of the piece —"Air Dancer."

Already she had to fight back a thin haze of tears. Shaking her head, Gypsy began to read:

Once there lived a breed of gypsy fliers, daredevil pilots who possessed the spirit to bridge our oceans and make our world a smaller, more accessible place. Yet beyond all that stirred a humbler motive. To fly for the sake of flight. To take nourishment from the sky as a tree does from the earth.

Most of those early pioneers are gone now, but they've passed that spirit on. It surely lives in the heart and mind of Erin "Gypsy" Gallagher, a native of Milwaukee, Wisconsin, and an annual participant in the Oshkosh air shows . . .

She skipped on ahead, past the family background, past the various trophies she'd won over the years at Fond du Lac. She hadn't realized until now just how good a writer Keane was, how shrewd an observer. For all his initial ignorance, he'd managed in the end to capture nuances even she'd been unaware of.

On the third page, in a blocked-off area near the bottom, she came upon an addition to the story. Though in smaller print, it nonetheless caught the eye with the caption, "Tragedy in Blakesburg: A Question of Guilt."

Gypsy's hands went cold.

It wasn't possible. Yet it was all there, in stark black and white. Lon's name, the accident, the investigation. And the rumors that flew, fast and furious through the air-show circuit. The whole nightmare, dredged up again for everyone to see, and to judge. At a time when she was finally ready to put it to rest and go forward.

She felt suddenly sick to her stomach. This must be the reason for Keane's reluctance to talk, and his insistence on keeping busy. He wanted to distract her, to stop her from seeing it. Perhaps he had regrets now that she'd come to him. He himself admitted that he thought she might have changed her mind. In the heat of anger and imagined rejection he probably fought back in the only way he knew how.

Am I trying to excuse him? she wondered. No, there could be no excuse for this. The man she'd claimed to love wouldn't have done it. Therefore, he couldn't be the man she'd thought he was. He'd taken her hard-earned trust and thrown it back in her face.

Later, the tears would come. Later, when the numbness wore off. And by then she'd be very far from here. She forced herself to stand, letting the magazine fall to the floor. The article no longer mattered, nor did the fact that thousands of people would read it. Only the betrayal seemed real—that, and the need to get away before Keane found her.

She packed only the things she'd brought with her and stole into an elevator just as the one beside it opened its doors. On the way down to the lobby she leaned against the wall and closed her eyes. The tears aren't supposed to come yet, she thought fiercely. Dammit, not yet. At least let me make it out of here in one piece. She needed strength now, not weakness. Not this sick feeling of hurt. She searched what remained of her "spirit," but came up empty.

"It was out of my hands, Keane. I wrote that side-bar before you even came back to New York, but I swear, I pulled it after our little 'discussion' that morning."

"Then what the hell happened, Paul?"

"Bitteman overruled me and put it back in, that's what happened. It's out on the newsstands today. I wanted to warn you before you brought out the assassins."

Keane stood near the back of the crowded elevator, hands buried in his pockets and head down as that telephone conversation played over and over through his mind. Oh, God, how was he going to explain it to Gypsy? Even *he* would have trouble believing the cockeyed story he had to lay on her.

The most important thing was that he reach her first, cockeyed story or no. Then it was up to her. *Dammit*, he should have seen this coming, but he'd been so blinded by his own emotions these past few weeks. That sidebar, however small, could do her, and Gallagher Aviation, irreparable damage, he knew. Not to mention totally destroy the trust they'd managed to build between themselves. It was his worst nightmare come to life—to have finally won her love, only to lose it before they'd had a chance to really experience it.

The doors slid open and he shoved his way to the front, oblivious to the angry protests he garnered. By the time he reached her suite he was nearly running. Though he tried to tell himself she couldn't possibly have seen the article yet, he felt an unfocused sense of panic.

The suite was empty.

"Gypsy?" he called as his eyes traveled aimlessly about the sitting room. "Kevin?"

On legs that didn't seem to be his own he walked into the bedroom. A white paper bag lay across the bed as if she'd tossed it there, then forgotten it. The closet door was open and her clothes and travel bag were gone.

Keane fought the groan that started in the pit of his stomach and worked its way up to his throat. On the bureau lay the silk scarf he'd bought her, all neat and folded. And on the bathroom floor he saw the edge of a discarded magazine.

He sank down on the bed, burying his face in his hands.

"Dad?" Kevin asked from the doorway connecting the two suites. "Are you in here?"

"In the bedroom," he mumbled.

His son entered and glanced around. "I'm hungry. Where's Gypsy?"

Keane lifted his head long enough to shake it. "I don't know."

"Maybe she went back down to find you."

"Oh, I doubt that, Kev. I seriously doubt that."

CHAPTER

Eight

"WELL, HERE SHE IS, just like I told you. All gassed up and ready to hit the sky."

Gypsy followed an unusually subdued Billie into a small private hangar on the Ottawa airfield. As soon as the older woman turned on a light her spirits lifted. The Moth's familiar vivid yellow was like a candle in the darkness—the one constant in her life that could always be counted on. "I'm as ready as she is," she said. "How much do I owe you for the gas and the space, Billie?"

"Let's see, for two days . . ." Billie gave her gray-blond head an abrupt shake. "I said before you wouldn't owe me for the space, and I mean to keep my word on that. Just bring me up even on the gas, and we'll be square."

Gypsy tore her eyes away from the Moth. "Is something wrong? The other night you were willing to fly me to Chicago, round up a justice of the peace, and buy me a wedding bouquet."

"The other night you struck me as a loner in need of a swift kick in the right direction. Two days later you come back famous. I guess you didn't need this old bird's help after all."

"What . . . ?" Gypsy cocked her head, puzzled.

"But you can't have read the article yet. I only saw it myself today."

"It just so happens, I subscribe to *World View*, girlie." She shifted her stance at Gypsy's stare, arms akimbo on her work-streaked brown flight suit. "I subscribe to a whole passel of magazines. That particular one was already in the mailbox waiting for me when we taxied down that runway out there."

So, it had begun, sooner than she expected, and from a surprising source. Yet the unspoken accusation sparked an emotion within Gypsy that she couldn't have anticipated. Anger. Pure, simple, and not peppered with guilt. A long-dead defense mechanism sprang into sudden, full-blown life. "And it's changed your outlook, hmm? Instead of a romantic heroine, I've become an accessory in my own husband's death." She laughed. "Keane tried to warn me about the power of the media."

"Power, hell. I'm no judge," Billie told her. "I leave that to others. I read those things, and after what you'd said about that journalist of yours, I . . . well, I put two and two together. I figured you'd be back here sooner than you should."

Gypsy let out a long slow breath. "It, uh . . . it was a mistake from the beginning. I should have trusted my instincts, but I didn't, and now I'll have to live with the consequences. But I won't live with the blame. Not anymore. For the record, Billie, I was not negligent five years ago. I was not responsible for my husband's accident."

"Then I'm not the one you need to fight."

"Right now the only thing I need is to go home." She stowed her bag in the Moth, then began a swift but thorough preflight check of the exterior.

"They say home is where the heart is." Billie watched her for a time, then waved a hand. "But then, I'm no preacher, either."

Half an hour later Gypsy was alone in the night sky. Her summer idyll had reached an abrupt end. Now it was more important than ever that she return to Gallagher Aviation. Whatever came about as a result of the article, she'd have to stand by Neal, and he her. Besides, the magic had gone out of the season. The magic had gone out of a lot of things. It was time to come down to earth, both literally and figuratively. Time for her to realize that dreams, like people, were sometimes as insubstantial and as shifting as the clouds.

Billie was wrong. It wasn't Keane that she needed to fight, but someone else . . .

Keane motioned to Kevin, then sauntered into one of the several hangars located at Milwaukee's Shorewood Air Park. "Uh, this is Gallagher Aviation, isn't it?" he asked a lone mechanic hard at work beneath the cowling of a single-engine Cessna.

The man straightened, revealing a red T-shirt identical to the one Gypsy had worn that day in the corn field. "You're in the right place. What can I do for you?"

Keane smiled, he hoped nonchalantly. "Is Gypsy around anywhere? She told me to meet her here at noon."

The mechanic took a long hard look at him before answering, "No, she isn't here."

Here we go again, thought Keane. Just like in Oshkosh. Why is everyone she works with so damned protective of her? Maybe they're trying to protect her from types like you, a part of him responded. And with good reason. "Oh." He pretended to glance at his watch. "I guess I am a little early, at that. I was supposed to talk to her about flying lessons for my son here, and I'm afraid I'm pressed for time."

Kevin emerged from around the corner of the hangar and the man's eyes narrowed. "Mister, I don't know what Gypsy told you, but minimum age for a pilot's license is sixteen."

"Of course, I'm aware of that, but I thought it wouldn't hurt to check into it while he still has a few years to change his mind." Keane leaned forward and added in confidential tones, "Actually, his mother and I are against it, but his grandfather, the police commissioner, well...he insisted. A flying buff from way back, you know. Is there anyone else here that I can talk to?"

The mechanic looked again at Kevin, who shrugged and grinned.

"Neal's in the office," he said slowly. "But I think he's busy on the phone."

"Neal! Sounds like just the man for me. You wait out here, son, I think this is one conversation you shouldn't be hearing. Is that the office over there?"

"Yeah..."

"Thanks so much, you've been a great help." Before the mechanic could say anything further Keane was knocking on the frosted glass door.

"Come!" shouted a gruff voice from inside.

He entered a small, surprisingly neat office space, and found it dominated by a large man in his midsixties who still possessed a wealth of graying black hair and eyes the color of a dusky sky.

The man stood and offered his hand. "Neal Gallagher. Was it flight instruction I heard you mention outside, or was it wishful thinkin' on my part?"

Keane took the hand and watched as it devoured his own. "Actually, sir, my name is Keane McCready. Your man seemed a little suspicious, so I—"

"Keane McCready, is it?" His eyes turned from blue to dark gray in a matter of moments, but the telephone interrupted his next comment. He answered it, then made short dispatch of whoever was on the other end. "Blasted phone hasn't quieted since yesterday. I suppose it's you I should be thankin' for that."

"Mr. Gallagher, if you'll spare me a few minutes, I'll try to explain what happened. Then if you want to kick me out, feel free."

After a weighted pause, Gypsy's father-in-law motioned for him to sit down. The telephone jangled again and without ceremony he took it off the hook, placing the receiver atop a dog-eared copy of *World View* magazine. "Talk, my lad, while you still have a tongue to do it."

Twenty-five minutes and several thousand words later, Keane sat back and waited for the verdict.

Gallagher regarded him with a strange kind of sadness, then shook his head. "Gypsy's had her share of troubles for such a young woman, but this . . . She's been so very quiet since she came back."

"So she is here. I didn't see her biplane outside, and I wondered if I'd been given the wrong information."

"Since late last night, yes. The Moth's over at Bixby's, gettin' a wax job."

Keane swallowed. "And where is Gypsy?" he asked.

"Around and about. I didn't press her to come to work her first day home, but I expect she'll be showin' herself soon enough."

"Then I'll wait, if you don't mind." He yawned and rubbed at his eyes. "I'm sorry, I didn't get much in the way of sleep last night."

"You're welcome to stretch out on the couch for a bit, if you like," Gallagher offered.

"Thanks, but I brought my son Kevin with me . . ."

The older man nodded. "I'm not sayin' I approve entirely of the way you've handled matters thus far, but I'd have to be a thick-headed fool not to see that you love her, lad. I'm goin' against her wishes lettin' you stay. I only hope it's for the better."

"I understand. Thank you for giving me the benefit of the doubt on this."

"You've told me the truth, haven't you?"

"Of course."

"Then why should I doubt you? And why should you thank me for acceptin' the truth?"

Keane chuckled. "You know, related or not, you and Gypsy are a lot alike. I can see where she gets her stubbornness."

"Naturally we're alike. And naturally we're stubborn. We're Irish!"

"I'll try to remember that."

They remained silent for a time, then Gallagher sobered. "Before Gypsy comes in and starts tearin' you limb from limb, I think we should have ourselves a bit of a talk . . . about what really happened to my son."

"Really, sir, you don't have to go into it. Gypsy already told me more than I had a right to know."

"And Gypsy's just lately realized a great deal more. Your article isn't the only thing she's had to adjust to."

Keane sat up straighter in his chair. "I'm listening."

"It's funny," Gypsy began with a faint smile. "I came here today to give you a piece of my mind, and now I don't feel a thing. No, that's not quite true. I feel some sadness, and some regret. Maybe even a little pity. But no anger . . . and no grief. Not anymore."

She lifted her head and listened to the birdsong that echoed through the trees. Strange that even in the middle of the busiest cities, cemeteries always managed to retain their quiet tranquility. Fresh flowers had recently been placed on Lon's grave, probably by Neal. He continued to make weekly visits like clockwork, but this was the first time Gypsy had come here in more than four and a half years. She'd always lacked the courage. Until now.

Weary of standing, she knelt in the thick grass. "I met someone this summer, Lon. For a while I thought I'd really found something to hang on to. Something . . . real. I don't think he meant to lie to me, but that doesn't take away the hurt. I had to leave because I knew I'd never be able to trust him again. Trust has been our major stumbling block. Trust, and my memories of you. I suppose my relationship with Keane was doomed from the start.

You know the saying about oil and water. But he did make me realize that I'd put our marriage on a kind of pedestal. I saw you the way I wanted to see you—the perfect husband, the perfect partner."

Her voice caught, yet she forced herself to go on. "But you weren't, were you? You were human, just like the rest of us. You had your good days, and your bad. You were capable of making mistakes, and errors in judgment. Just like us . . ."

"Then the faulty fuel pump *wasn't* the cause of your son's accident?" Keane asked in confusion.

Neal rubbed his forehead and sighed. "I suspect none of us will ever really know for certain."

"But . . . Gypsy told me the FAA ruling stated—"

"She told you that because it's what she wanted to believe, lad. I have copies of the final determination right here, if you'd care to see them. *Inconclusive*." He stood and began to pace the small office. "Inconclusive. That pump might indeed have carried a manufacturer's defect, in which case no mechanic could've found it. But the fact remains, no pilot in his right mind would put a craft of that sort through the kind of maneuver he did, on a simple *test* flight."

Keane felt uncomfortable watching the large man dodge his chair on every turn, so he too stood. "Then what you're saying is—"

"What I'm sayin', is that if the blame for Lon's death should fall anywhere, most likely it should fall on Lon himself. I don't pretend to know what he felt that morning. Perhaps he wanted to prove somethin' to Gypsy because of some silly quarrel they'd had the night before. In any case, he played the fool, and I'd have told him so myself if he'd come out of it alive."

"I'm sorry," Keane said softly.

"Oh, don't get me wrong. I loved my son. Maybe that's why I was able to look the truth in the face. That one mistake, however fatal it proved to be, didn't alter my love."

"Not like it must have altered Gypsy's," Keane added, completing the thought. "No wonder she got so angry with me every time I tried to punch holes in her storybook memories."

"No wonder Keane got so frustrated with me every time we tried to talk," Gypsy said with a rueful smile. "I'm surprised he *kept* trying. *He* made me see that I'd been lying to myself all those years, even before I called Neal. He made me see so many things, and then he pulled the rug out from underneath. Oh, God, Lon, how can I go back to that same life again? I've changed. He's changed me. And I know that I don't want to be alone anymore."

She stood on cramped legs and brushed off her jeans. "Well, I guess I've said what I came here to say. You're a better listener now than you were when we were married, I'll give you that." Slowly she pulled a long piece of torn and soiled white silk from her pocket, then placed it beside Neal's colorful flowers. "I won't be needing this from now on. The other one, either. Sometimes you have to leave certain things behind you in order to say good-bye. Good-bye, Lon."

* * *

"Dammit, Neal, I am not going to make it easy for her to just walk away from me. I deserve better than 'So long, sucker.'" Now it was Keane who paced Gallagher's office, while Gallagher himself prepared two paper cups of coffee.

"Perhaps your boy would like soda. You may both be in for a long wait."

"What? Oh." Keane stopped long enough to check his watch. "Could she have gone home, do you think? Maybe I could find her there."

"Gypsy, at home?" The older man laughed. "The only time she's ever at home is for a change of clothes and an occasional meal. Not one for stayin' on the same perch for long, our girl."

"Born to the wanderlust," Keane murmured.

"That she is. Just like her father, and his father before him. The O'Haras always were a skittish lot."

"So I've learned."

"Come, let's get some air. And I'd like to meet that boy of yours. Kevin, is it?"

"Right." Keane grabbed his coffee and followed him out into the hangar.

Kevin stood on a stepladder, head bent over the Cessna's engine, while the hapless mechanic tried to keep up with his rapid-fire questions.

Gallagher smiled and started to join them, but Keane put a hand on his arm. "Was it the FAA report that started the rumors circulating around your son's death?" he asked.

"Later on, maybe, when the reporters got to diggin'. Most likely it was a few so-called friends who surrounded Lon and Gypsy at the time and saw what happened. Why? Is it important?"

"It may be. I'll need to talk to some of those 'friends' when I do my follow-up story."

"Follow-up?" Gallagher turned to look at him, eyes guarded. "For *World View*?"

"Uh-uh. As of yesterday, I became free-lance. Just one more question, sir. If I can clear Gypsy's name in print, would you be averse to my using what you've just told me?"

"Everything?"

"Within reason."

It didn't take the man as long as Keane thought it might to reach a decision. "Our greatest concern should be for the living. The truth can't hurt my son any more than it already has. Still, it's Gypsy's life and reputation, so I think you ought to put that question to her."

Keane nodded. "Thanks, I will. If she ever shows up. I'm beginning to think . . . ."

Gypsy heard voices as she neared Gallagher Aviation's open-ended hangar. Disturbingly familiar voices that made her want to turn and run for all she was worth in the opposite direction.

"Oh, Neal," she whispered. "You promised me you wouldn't see him if he came here."

What now, then? Do as her instincts dictated and flee? The coward's way out, a part of her chided. I thought I was determined to be stronger than that from here on in.

She stood to the side of the structure, waging a small but intense war with her emotions, for close to five minutes. Then she took a deep breath and went in, trying her best to feel only the anger and humiliation Keane's words had put her through. The hurt and betrayal she'd keep to herself. Those particular feelings were too new. Too painful.

Keane had his back to her, as did Neal. The two seemed involved in deep conversation, when suddenly Keane broke off midsentence. His back stiffened just before he turned and met her eyes.

For an elongated few seconds they simply stared at one another. Then Kevin followed his father's gaze and jumped off his stepladder, breaking the strained silence. "Gypsy! We've been waiting for you forever. Where were you?"

She couldn't help but smile at his enthusiasm, opening her arms as the boy came to her. "Visiting someone," she told him. "How're you doing, smart guy?"

"I'm okay," he said, reluctant to leave her embrace. "It's Dad who's a mess again. Why didn't you just tell him you wanted to come home early?"

Gypsy winced. She hadn't thought about how her sudden departure might have affected Kevin. "It's . . . kind of complicated," she confessed. "Why don't you let Neal show you around the air park so your dad and I can talk about it." She looked to her father-in-law, who watched her closely.

"You'll be all right?" he asked.

"Yes."

It was obvious Kevin wanted to stay with them, but Neal managed to coax him away for a tour of the field. John, their second mechanic, beat a hasty retreat into the offices for a long coffee break.

The silence returned once she and Keane were left alone. Gypsy tried to look everywhere but at his face, afraid of what she might read there. It was a losing battle, though, because his features held her eyes like a magnet. "How did you know I was here?" she asked at last.

"I had a beer and a long talk with Billie at the Final Approach in Ottawa."

She nodded. "I should have guessed. You do that sort of thing for a living, after all."

"Gypsy, I—" He took a step forward.

"Don't," she warned sharply.

"Okay."

"Just stay back."

"I said okay."

"Fine."

After another thirty-second silence he sighed in exasperation. "This is ridiculous."

"You're right."

"I thought you wanted to talk."

"Is your notebook handy? You wouldn't want to miss anything." Her nails dug into her palms, but she couldn't seem to unclench her hands. If she did, the anger might subside.

Keane pointed a finger at her. "You are impossible."

"And you don't know when to stop pushing your luck."

"This is luck? You're not even going to try to listen to me, are you?"

"I think I've heard it all before."

"No—"

"Just leave me alone, Keane."

"No."

She closed her eyes. "You shouldn't have come here."

"I had to."

"It's over."

"It hasn't even started yet, Gypsy."

"It was finished *before* it started."

"You're wrong!" he shouted.

"And you lied to me!"

This time their harsh breathing filled the sudden quiet.

Gypsy turned away so he wouldn't see the tear that tracked down her cheek. She fought to get the anger back, but the hurt was taking control. Not so surprising, really, since it was the stronger of the two.

Behind her, Keane moved—farther back. "I have never lied to you," he said, almost in an undertone.

"There're different ways to lie. One is by ommission. I'd say you fall into that category. You knew all along that side piece was going to be printed, yet you chose not to tell me. When did you write it, Keane? When you convinced yourself I wouldn't come to Chicago?"

"My God. You actually believe that, don't you?"

"I didn't want to believe it," she told him. "But the evidence was more than a little...overwhelming."

He began to pace the concrete floor, and his footsteps echoed in the cavernous hangar. "I didn't write that sidebar. Daniels slipped it through without my permission..." He hesitated. "What 'evidence'?"

"It doesn't really matter now, does it?"

"Oh, wonderful. Tell me something, does our relationship mean so little to you that you're not even willing to consider my explanation? After all we've been through, do you think you can afford to just throw it away like this?"

The more strident his voice became, the more of an effort it required for Gypsy to keep a lid on her own emotions. She turned around to find him standing, hands in his pockets and one foot on the stepladder Kevin had vacated, looking as though he'd been through as great an ordeal as she had in the past twenty-four hours. "You could have warned me, Keane. If you'd come to me with your explanations *before* the article was printed, things might have been different."

"How many ways do I have to say it? I didn't know it was in there myself until I found the magazine on your bathroom floor! That's what that phone call was about. Daniels was warning *me*."

After a moment Gypsy began to laugh.

"What the hell's so funny?" he demanded.

"I don't know, that's what's funny. I don't know anymore whether you're telling me the truth or manipulating me. Maybe you've been manipulating me all along, huh? That'd really be hilarious."

"You know better than that, Gypsy."

"Do I?"

"Yes, you do." He came to her and lifted her chin with his fingertips.

She tried not to pull away.

"I am deeply sorry about what happened. If I hadn't been so preoccupied with my feelings for you I might have seen it coming and stopped it in time. As it is, all I can do is try my best to make it up to you. Tell me it isn't too late to do that."

His touch, his very nearness, threatened to undo her more than his anger had. That, and the way he looked at her, with those enigmatic, sky-colored eyes. He could probably charm a flea off a dog if he set his mind to it. "I'm sorry, too," she told him. "But I just don't know if I can believe you."

"Then we're at a stalemate."

"I guess we are."

They didn't move, merely stared at one another for several seconds, then Keane slowly dropped his hand.

John chose that moment to reenter the hangar, clutching a half-eaten sandwich. "I, uh, don't mean to interrupt you two, but I thought you should know—"

Gypsy stepped away from Keane and pushed a strand of hair from one eye. "What is it, John?"

"That little boy that was here? I just saw him get onto a city bus across the street."

"What?" Keane shook his head in confusion. "I thought he went with Gallagher."

"He did," Gypsy hastened to assure him. "It must have been some other boy."

"No, ma'am," said the mechanic. "He was wearing a long-sleeved blue shirt and tan trousers, right?"

Gypsy's heart began to thud hard in her chest, but before either she or Keane had a chance to answer, Neal hurried into the hangar.

"Did Kevin come back here?" he asked them all. "I thought I saw him headin' this way a few minutes ago."

Keane's face drained of color as he swore under his breath and ran full out for the street exit.

"Neal, what happened?" Gypsy clutched at his

arm and tried not to panic. The apprehension in Keane's eyes had scared her.

"I should be askin' you that question. The lad said he wanted to go get a drink of water. I waited over by Bixby's, but he didn't come back."

"Oh, no. He probably overheard Keane and me shouting at each other."

"He's not the only one. I'll wager the entire airfield managed to hear most of it."

Keane returned from the bus stop, out of breath. "It's long gone. I'm going to need a bus schedule to know where it's headed."

"I think I have one in my office," Gypsy told him. "Follow me. Keane, why in the world would he take off like that?"

He glanced at her, but didn't slow his stride as she led him to her small cubicle just down the hall from Neal's. "I haven't told you everything there is to know about Kevin. This isn't the first time he's run away. It's happened twice before. I thought he was over it. *Dammit*, he doesn't even know this city."

"We'll find him," Gypsy promised, though she didn't feel as confident as she sounded. Whatever she and Keane's differences, they'd have to be put aside now, because she wasn't about to let him search for his son alone. Regardless of her feelings for his father, she'd come to love Kevin, and she was partly to blame for his running away.

After all, she'd set him a fine example in Chicago, hadn't she?

CHAPTER
Nine

STRANGE THE WAY ONE'S dreams were sometimes fullfilled. Only yesterday Keane would have given anything to be strapped in the front cockpit of the Moth again, with Gypsy calm and confident behind him. Now, as they glided low over a checkerboard of farm fields on the far outskirts of Milwaukee, he wished with all his soul that this trip hadn't been necessary.

Two hours had passed since Kevin stepped onto a bus bound for Greendale, southwest of town. He hadn't arrived. According to the driver, whom the police contacted by radio, the boy had disappeared when the bus developed a flat tire on an isolated country road. Milwaukee's finest could spare only two cars and a lone helicopter to canvass the area, so Gypsy had volunteered to use the Moth, keeping in close contact with those on the ground via her own radio. So far, not a sign.

Keane's eyes swept over every inch of the fields below. He wondered if it was even possible to see a small boy down there from their distance. His head ached. It would be dark soon, and they'd have to stop for the night. Valuable time lost.

He twisted around to look at Gypsy and threw up his hands.

She nodded and circled lower, but she was limited by power lines. It was the best she could do.

Back at Gallagher Aviation she'd been all business, possessing a cooler head than he. Only once had she taken him aside and asked, "Do you think we should call Kevin's mother?"

"No. Absolutely not. Not yet, anyway. There's no sense putting her through hell tonight when she can't do anything."

"I suppose you're right."

He'd started to say something further, about how much he appreciated her concern and her help, but she turned away from him to begin her preflight on the Moth. So, he thought. This is how it's going to be. The solicitous stranger, ever willing to aid a person in need. If not me, then somebody else. After all, what's the difference, right?

They stayed up for another half hour, then Gypsy brought them gently down in a field of wild grass. Keane experienced that familiar sense of weightlessness just before they touched the ground. Then, earthbound once more, he finally realized what it must be like for her. His body felt leaden, his mind heavy and numb. In the sky, in that open space where anything seemed possible, he'd held on to his hope. Now this field acted like a magnet, slowing his movement and sapping his mental strength.

After Gypsy killed the engine he removed his goggles, undid his belt, then hoisted himself from the biplane. "Why did we land?"

Gypsy, still seated, removed her own goggles and studied him as he walked about to stretch his legs.

"We'll spend the night here," she told him matter-of-factly. "It'll save us travel time in the morning, and as soon as the sun comes up we'll pick up where we left off. I brought food, water, and bedrolls."

He helped her unload their supplies, one ear cocked to the radio she'd left on. Its faint static was the only audible sound for miles. He'd grown unaccustomed to the quiet in these past few weeks.

Once they'd positioned everything to her satisfaction, Gypsy began to heat a large can of beef stew.

The aroma only served to nauseate him, so Keane turned away and walked to the nose of the plane. The brilliant pink-and-orange sunset brought back memories of the one that evening, a little over three weeks ago, when Gypsy's unique magic had first woven its tendrils through his awareness.

So much gained in so little time, and so much lost. He couldn't lose Kevin too. Dear God, he couldn't lose his son this way.

"You should eat something," Gypsy said, wincing at the intrusive sound of her own soft voice.

From his position near the Moth's stilled propeller, Keane half turned. "I'm...not really hungry, thanks."

"You'll be no good to Kevin if you starve yourself."

"I said, I'm not hungry," he snapped.

Stung despite herself, Gypsy lowered her head to the food. In truth, she wasn't hungry either, but it was something to do—something to keep her hands occupied and her mind still, if only for a short while. Then what? She felt as if they were both walking a tightrope, afraid to look down, each intent on avoiding the other even though they were suspended on the same taut wire.

"We'll find him, Keane," she tried again. "He can't have gotten far. Maybe a family took him in. It's only a matter of time before the police knock on the right door."

"Someone could have picked him up on the road," he muttered. "It happens all the time. He could be halfway to the state line by now."

"We're not in New York or Chicago," she reminded him. "This is farm country. I know a lot of the people who live out here, and they're warm and decent. Kevin couldn't have chosen a more hospitable place to run to, believe me."

He grunted once, then fell silent. The sun had fallen lower on the flat horizon, silhouetting him in much the same way it had her in the photograph he'd stolen a small lifetime ago.

Gypsy ached to go to him, to wrap her arms around him. To comfort him. But even under these circumstances she couldn't just forget. Too much had happened. Too much had changed. She forced herself to take a few bites of the stew, then put it aside to make some coffee. She doubted either one of them would get much sleep tonight, anyway.

The aroma finally drew him back from his solitary vigil, and he came to sit on the other side of the stove, opposite her.

She handed him a cup and he took it with a grateful sigh. "Thanks."

"If you'd rather not go into this, just say so," she started on a tentative note. "But I'd like to know why Kevin ran away the other times. It might help us to find him now."

He took a deep breath and lifted his eyes to her. Even in the waning light she could see they were red-rimmed and sunken. Was Kevin's disappearance the sole cause?

"The last time was two years ago," he said, voice low. "Beth was frantic. Luckily I was home when she called me. Kev's hamster had just died, and he'd gone in search of a pet cemetery; at least that's what he told the police when they found him five hours later. He'd managed to get pretty far from home, and he was only six then. God knows what might have happened to him if they hadn't gotten to him before dark."

"And the first?"

"A few months before that. He'd just spent the weekend with me. I guess he didn't want it to end, because less than two hours after I dropped him home, a cabby delivered him back to the door of my apartment. I'd moved recently, but even so, he'd memorized my new address. I mean, can you believe it? At six!"

"I believe it." She observed the way his face came alive, as it did whenever he talked about his son, and decided to break a confidence. "He's a genius, Keane."

He tried to smile. "Yeah. A chip off the old block."

"I'm serious. He swore me to secrecy, but I think you have a right to know. Kevin is a very gifted child, and you have every reason to be proud."

"If that's the case, then why did he do a damned-fool thing like get on that bus?" He stood suddenly, too agitated to remain seated for long.

"I don't know. But regardless of his IQ, he's still a little boy, with little-boy emotions. That's what he doesn't want us to lose sight of."

He didn't say anything for a while, merely stood and watched as dusk slowly faded into night. Then he shook his head. "How could I have *not* known?" he whispered. "He's shown me in a thousand different ways. What's he showing me now, Gypsy? What is he trying to tell me?"

"I don't think it's you this time. It's me." She lit the lantern and placed it between them. That only occupied her for a few moments and soon she forced herself to look up and meet his bewildered gaze. "Don't you see? I meant to walk out on you in Chicago, but I walked out on Kevin, too. He opened up to me, yet I was willing to leave without a single look back. He's probably afraid I'll do it again."

"Will you?" he asked.

She knew there was no avoiding the question. Just like the sun, it was bound to come up sooner or later. Why couldn't it be later, then, when her head felt clearer and Kevin was safely back in his father's care? "I don't think now is the time . . ." she began.

"Oh, and when do you suppose the right time will come, hmm? Tomorrow? The next day? Or maybe never. You're very good at probing other people's psyches—are you so blind to your own that you can't see you're doing the same thing *he* is?"

Gypsy's mouth dropped open at his words. It seemed she'd opened Pandora's box, and judging from the state Keane was in, who knew where his anger might lead them both. "I don't—"

"You're still running away!"

He advanced on her, and she saw that strange, gilt-edged glitter come into his eyes.

"Chicago was a prime example," he continued. "Typical Gypsy Gallagher. You read that article and *boom*—the decision was made. Without thought to the consequences, without even giving me a chance to explain myself, you took off! What I want to know is, when are you gonna land? I mean, don't you ever get tired up there all alone, flapping your wings against the wind and anybody else who happens to remind you you're a living, breathing woman? Maybe your love was too much to ask for, but whatever happened to trust?"

"I *did* trust you!"

"Past tense?" He made a conscious effort to lower his voice as he stood over her. "You bestowed your trust on me, Gypsy, like some gift from the gods. You never gave me a chance to earn it."

She stared at him, then stood herself, ducking out of his reach when he made a grab for her. Once outside the circle of lantern light she filled her lungs with cool fresh air. "It always comes back to the same old argument, doesn't it?" she asked. "For what it's worth, I'm beginning to believe you about the article. No one would put up this much of a fight to defend a lie."

"Why, thank you, Saint Gypsy." He gave her a mock bow from the center of the lantern's glow, a reluctant actor in a spotlight that revealed more than he intended. "See what I mean?"

"You're upset, and you're dead tired, Keane. We

can talk about this after we've found Kevin, all right?"

"No, not all right."

Gypsy closed her eyes. "Look, I'm sick of fighting you, and I haven't had the best of days myself. We both need some rest—"

"You haven't forgotten what we shared in Chicago, have you? And surely you haven't forgotten this." Slowly he pulled the white silk scarf he'd bought her from his jacket pocket. "I guess you left it behind in your hurry."

He held it out to her and she couldn't stop the sudden rush of tears that clouded her vision.

"Take it," he urged. "It belongs to you. I, uh . . . all the way to Milwaukee I kept replaying this scene over and over in my head. I'd get to this point, and no further. Like writer's block. Would you take it, or would you tell me where I could put it? I honestly didn't know. I still don't. All I have left to say is I love you, Gypsy. If that's not good enough, tell me, once and for all, and I'll back off."

Gypsy felt a peculiar sense of déjà vu as she watched her hand reach out, seemingly of its own volition. She remembered what she'd said at Lon's grave earlier that day, and the words still held true.

"I've changed . . . he's changed me. I don't want to be alone anymore."

At last her fingers touched the soft silk. Keane let go of the scarf and it cascaded over her hands like a stream of cool water. After a moment she brought it to her cheek and whispered, "I'm sorry."

He took her into his arms as though she were some delicate creature he couldn't bear to crush.

"I'm not asking for apologies," he told her, his breath warm and welcome on her hair.

She accepted the comfort of his embrace, and tried to give a little of that comfort back. Lord knew, it was what both of them needed most at the moment. Whether or not they'd solved anything remained to be seen.

Strangely, it was Keane who pulled away first. An odd shyness seemed to come over him, as if he felt embarrassed about his earlier outburst.

"I'll...go lay out the bedrolls," Gypsy said softly.

He nodded.

The silence that settled between them as she worked was a different kind of silence this time. Not strained and heavy, but lighter...easier somehow. When she was finished she beckoned him over. "Lie down. Try to get some rest; we've got a hard day ahead of us tomorrow."

He sighed and did as she suggested, stretching out atop one of the bedrolls fully clothed. She could see how taut his muscles remained and knew it would be quite a while before he was relaxed enough to fall asleep.

"Where are you going?" he asked when she started toward the cockpit.

"To check in with Neal one more time. Let him know we're okay."

He settled back again, hands behind his head, and watched her.

She returned a couple of minutes later, after a clipped, uninformative conversation. She read the question in Keane's eyes as she bent to extinguish the lantern. "No news," she told him.

The night air had grown a little chill, so she zipped her jacket and wound the scarf around her neck a few times for added warmth. She continued to feel his eyes on her in the darkness. As her own sight adjusted to the dim moonlight the outline of his body became visible. He hadn't moved.

"Gypsy?" he whispered.

"Hmm?"

He shifted, reaching out to her. "I need you."

Slowly she knelt, and didn't protest when he pulled her down beside him. She rested her head on his chest and heard his heartbeat, a steady, reassuring sound.

"Just hold me," he said. "And don't let go."

It wasn't difficult to do. Gypsy wrapped her arms around him and held on tight.

They remained that way until well into the night, both awake, yet both content to simply hold and be held by the other. Back under the Moth's protective wing. Back where it all started.

Until Gypsy spoke into the stillness. "I do love you, Keane."

His breathing seemed to stop for a moment, before he lifted her head and sought her lips with his. "Then there's gotta be a future."

Despite her ever-present fear for Kevin, Gypsy eventually sank into a deep sleep against Keane's warm chest. His words followed her down. *There's gotta be a future. Gotta be. A future . . .*

"Ladies and gentlemen," said a faceless announcer to the huge crowd gathered beneath a perfect dream of a sky. "I now present to you, the winners of this year's Shorewood Air Park aerobatics competition—sponsored of course by Gallagher Aviation—Gypsy and Keane McCready, otherwise known as, the Clashing McCreadys!"

Gypsy nudged Keane, who, dressed in a spotless white flight suit identical to hers, yawned as a din of wild applause broke out around them. "Smile, darling."

He raised a hand to their enthusiastic audience. "Really, dear, this gets a little tedious. After all, we've managed to nab first place every year for the past three decades. Isn't it about time we retired, like normal, self-respecting sixty-five-year-olds?"

"Speak for yourself," she snapped. "If you remember, *I'm* still on the shy side of sixty."

The applause waned at long last, and she stepped to the microphone to take questions from the myriad reporters gathered just below the podium.

"*New York Times*, Mrs. McCready," a man near the center spoke up. "Considering your famous de-Havilland Moth is nearly a hundred years old, how do you keep it in such excellent condition?"

Gypsy acknowledged his compliment with a gracious nod. "I learned a long time ago that a little tender loving care will keep almost anything in top form. Isn't that right, sweetheart?"

"Oh, absolutely, absolutely," Keane said, putting his arm around her waist.

"Then why are you called 'the Clashing McCreadys'?" asked a young woman with a notepad.

Gypsy started to answer, but Keane whispered, "I'll take this one," and leaned toward the mike.

"Because, my dear, aside from the aforementioned TLC, my lovely wife and I hardly ever agree on anything. Come around to our place on a typical Sunday afternoon, and you'll see what I—"

Gypsy brought her foot down on top of his, which effectively silenced him. "That's not true," she countered.

"Of course it is," he said with a grimace.

"No, it isn't."

"Excuse me." Another woman raised her hand. Beside her stood a cameraman, ready to roll. "WLSX, Milwaukee. Mr. McCready, your son Kevin is a leading astrophysicist, your own memoirs have reached the top of the best-seller lists, and your wife's feats are legendary. How do you account for your family's phenomenal success, especially, if you'll pardon me, at your age?"

"Yes, amazing, isn't it?" He patted Gypsy's shoulder with affection. "After all those legendary feats, she still doesn't look a day over thirty." He lifted a strand of her hair. "More than a bit gray, maybe, but in direct sunlight you can still see a hint of that luscious auburn she used to hawk in those long-ago shampoo ads."

"Paul Daniels, Jr., *The National Inquisitor*, Mr. and Mrs. McCready. How is it your marriage has lasted all these years?"

Gypsy pried the microphone from Keane's hand. "I'll take this one, darling." She looked out over the hushed spectators and smiled. "Keane and I have had our trials and tribulations, but trust has always seen us through thick and thin. Well, trust and a new silk scarf now and again. Yes, indeed, the day I saved my husband's life was the luckiest day of mine."

Keane turned to her and grinned. His dimples were a little deeper, but that imp still lived behind his sky-blue eyes. As long as it remained, she knew their life together would never be boring.

"One more question, folks, before the parade. Any future plans?"

"As a matter of fact," Gypsy answered, "we've bought some property on the outskirts of town. It has this huge old barn, and Kevin's offered to help us renovate it . . ."

Gypsy sighed and turned over in her sleep. She always did like parades. But *barns*?

Keane felt Gypsy moving away from him, so he reached out to draw her back . . .

. . . and encountered the wooden arm of her chair as she rocked it to and fro. As in all his dreams, the setting was etched in vivid detail, from the hard wood of their spacious front porch to the sound of crickets chirping in a nearby copse of trees.

"Ahh," he sighed in perfect contentment. "Hasn't it been wonderful, spending the autumn of our lives here in this house in the country, far from the madding crowd . . . Gypsy, my pet, slow down your rocking, will you, you're making me nauseous."

"Oh, sorry, dear." She looked up from her knitting and smiled. "I suppose I still have a smidgen of the wanderlust left in me, even if I don't make it off the porch."

"Yes, I'm sure if that rocker only had wings, you'd pilot it to California and back. What's that you're knitting, by the way?"

Proudly she held it up for his inspection. "It's a scarf for Kevin's new daughter."

Keane cleared his throat. "I'm sure it's very nice, but don't you think two weeks old is a little young for something so long?"

"She'll grow into it soon enough. You know how I like to keep busy."

"Please, don't remind me. In this past week you've managed to install a satellite dish in our backyard, completely rewire the electrical system in our kitchen, and overhaul the engines of both our cars." He shook his head. "I mean, really, Gypsy, couldn't you take up canning like some of the other ladies in the neighborhood?"

"Poor Keane." She chuckled. "Are you sorry you've stayed with me all these years?"

"Of course not! The happiest years of my life have been the ones I've spent with you—traveling around the country in your biplane, starting a publishing business of my very own, raising a beautiful family."

"And you still have a lot to look forward to," she promised. "Like giving the barn a new coat of paint tomorrow morning."

He started to protest, but thought better of it. "See what I mean? A thrill a minute. There's one question I think it's time I asked you, though."

She peered at him over the rim of her spectacles. "Yes, dear?"

"Don't you think we ought to set the wedding date?"

"Don't rush me, Keane."

* * *

"I had a very weird dream just before you woke me up," Keane mentioned as they reloaded the Moth shortly after sunrise. "We were—"

"That's funny, so did I." Gypsy shook her head, then downed the last of her instant coffee. "I don't remember too much of it, but we were famous, and there was something to do with a barn. Crazy stuff. Must've been the beef stew."

"Must've been," he muttered, his thoughts already on the day ahead, and what it might bring. Then, several seconds later, one of her words belatedly caught his attention. "Did you say barn?"

She nodded as she began her usual painstaking preflight. "Yes, why?" When he didn't answer her she paused to look at him. "Is anything wrong?"

He turned around in a slow circle, gazing out over the flat midwestern horizon. "Is anything wrong?" he repeated, and laughed. "Oh my, no, what could be wrong?"

"I didn't mean . . ."

"I know, I know. Sorry. This may sound a little loony, but there was a barn in my dream, too. I was just wondering if that might mean something."

"Mean something?" She abandoned the Moth and came to place a hand on his shoulder. "We're not at the point where we need to grasp at straws, Keane. Look, I know this is tearing you apart, but we *will* find him. I know it."

"Do you?" Keane grimaced at the course of his own emotions. One minute he was up, the next down. The woman beside him had become his only stability, and he clung to her support. "If we don't find him by noon, I'll have to call Beth."

"We'll worry about that at noon," she told him.

"In the meantime, let's get up there and do what we can, okay? Come on."

As he strapped himself into the cockpit he couldn't help asking, "Last night, when you said you loved me . . . that wasn't just a Band-Aid, was it? I mean, to make me feel better just long enough—"

"No," came her simple reply as she lowered her goggles, and then the Moth fired up beneath them, leaving no more room for talk.

Keane felt that familiar lightness of spirit as soon as they were airborne, so he tried to still his mind and relax into it. They headed west, backs to the warming sunrise. The various houses and buildings below them were beginning to look more scattered as they moved farther away from town, and the land resembled a country quilt of brilliant September colors.

Kevin was down there, somewhere. Alone, or with strangers? Gypsy had contacted Neal before she was even awake enough to see. His voice, over the radio, had sounded gruff but optimistic, though there was nothing new to report from his end. No one had called the police during the night about a lost boy. Life, it seemed, was content to go on, irrespective of the gap that had opened up in his.

Twenty minutes later, Keane spotted it. A huge, ramshackle barn, off by itself at the side of a narrow dirt road. Surrounded by wild grass and foliage, it looked to have been abandoned for years. From the air it was possible to see burned remains of the house that had once stood nearby.

Even as he turned to gesture to Gypsy she was edging into a gentle descent. So, despite what she'd said, something about it struck a chord within her, too.

They circled the structure a couple of times, low enough for Keane to see the faded and peeling red paint on its sloped roof. He glanced back at Gypsy again, and she raised one shoulder as if to say, "Should we?"

The rules and limitations of civilization became moot once more. The world consisted of themselves, a bright yellow biplane, and what lay below. It was time to trust his instincts, the way he had before, because there was nothing out there to tell him otherwise.

Keane nodded, and held on as she circled one last time, then lined them up with the dirt road in preparation to land. It would be tricky, even he could see that. The road was uneven and rutted, but compared to the field beside it, it was the best they could hope for. He realized he was clutching the sides of the Moth with white-knuckled hands and willed himself not to shut his eyes when they touched down.

Gypsy's very bones began to rattle as soon as the landing gear made contact with solid ground. She'd come in slow, but that didn't stop the Moth from finding every last pothole and rock on its feeble excuse for a runway.

The barn loomed, solid and imposing, up ahead, and she applied the brakes sparingly so they wouldn't skew into the side of it before they came to a complete stop. Lord, she thought. This had better be worth it, because I don't know if I'll be able to get us back up again when it's all over.

She couldn't spare a glance to see how Keane was faring. It took every ounce of strength she possessed to keep hold of the stick and maintain some semblance of control. From the air, it hadn't looked quite this bad. Or had it? In her desire to help the man she loved find his son, might she have erred in judgment, even a little bit?

The right front tire blew as she braked one last time, and the slight skid it produced effectively brought them to a bumpy halt in a cloud of dust about a hundred yards past the barn. Gypsy killed the engine immediately and they sat in silence for a full minute before either of them dared to move. But that was okay. It gave her time to gather her wits, not to mention her thoughts.

At last Keane slowly unbuckled himself and turned around. Beneath his goggles, his face was chalk pale, and when he tried to smile, it came off a bit flat.

She wasn't sure if hers came off any better. "Definitely not one of my better landings," she said.

He cocked his head at that. "Funny. The Gypsy I used to know would have cashiered herself out of the pilots' union by now, if there was one."

She shrugged. "What can I say? I'm only human."

He stared at her for a moment. And when he smiled again she caught sight of the dimple. "Thank God for that. Welcome to the real world, Gypsy lady. I promise I won't hold it against you."

Gypsy took a deep breath and pushed her own goggles up. "Come on. Let's go check out that barn. I, for one, am anxious to find out what the attraction is."

She hoisted herself out of the Moth, and he followed suit, hurrying after her. From ground level, it looked even larger than it had from the air. It revealed its age in myriad ways. A broken metal weather vane, lying rusted and useless on the ground. A rotted wooden door that hung from equally rusted hinges, open to whoever and whatever deigned to enter.

Inside, it smelled damp and musty. Keane shook his head as they took a look around. "I can't imagine him coming into a place like this. At night, in the dark, it'd spook the hell out of *me*." In spite of those words, he cupped his hands around his mouth and called, "Kevin? It's Dad, are you in here?"

"Wait a minute." Gypsy squinted through the slanting sunlight. "I thought I heard something."

"What?"

"I'm not sure. A vagrant, maybe, or a stray animal. Who knows?" She stopped at the bottom of a wooden ladder that led to a darkened hayloft. "Up there."

"Uh-uh." Keane held her back. "Don't even think about it. I'll go."

"Don't be ridiculous, that ladder wouldn't support you. It may not even support me."

"But it could support an eight-year-old kid the size of a large postage stamp, right?"

He looked at her.

She looked at him.

"Spot me," she ordered, and started to climb before he talked her out of it. Surprisingly, the rungs held, so she made it to the top without mishap. It was dark, but she could tell very little straw remained on the hardwood flooring. Cautiously she made her way across it on her hands and knees.

"See anything?" Keane asked from below.

"Not yet." She heard the noise again, a soft scratching sound, and she froze. "Keane?"

"Yeah?"

"If a giant rat should come at me in the next few seconds, be prepared to catch me on the way down, okay?"

"*What?*"

Slowly but surely Gypsy's eyes began to adjust to the darkness, and she made out the top of what resembled a thatch of blond hair in the corner.

The thatch shifted as the boy beneath it awakened. "Gypsy?" he murmured, voice fuzzy with sleep.

She let out the breath she'd been holding. "Kevin McCready, am I glad to see you."

"Gypsy, please tell me what's happening," begged Keane.

Without hesitation the boy launched himself into her arms, and she held him, wanting to laugh and cry at the same time. Instead, she made herself call down to his father, "He's here, I've got him."

Evidently he noted the catch in her throat and believed her, because she heard him start for the ladder.

"No, don't," she warned. "We'll come to you." To Kevin she said, "If both of us made it up that rickety thing, I'm sure we can make it down. Sound logical enough?"

He nodded as he put on his glasses. "Dad's mad at me, isn't he?"

"More like scared to death," she told him. "But we'll talk about that later. Let's go. You first."

When Kevin was safely on the ground, she followed, skipping every other rung for fear that one might collapse under her. She felt Keane's strong hands about her waist when she neared the bottom, and jumped the last couple of feet. "Thanks. I never thought I'd be so happy to be back on terra firma."

Turning, she found that neither father nor son had made a move toward each other. They stood, eyes locked, until Kevin finally lowered his.

"I'm sorry I scared you," he said in a small voice.

All the anger seemed to go out of Keane, and he knelt. "I'm okay now. Just get over here, come on."

After only a slight pause, Kevin walked into his outstretched arms.

He held him tightly for a moment, as if to make sure he was really there. Then he took a good look at him. "You're all right?"

"Sure. A little hungry, is all."

"Then tell me why, Kev."

The boy glanced at Gypsy and she tried to smile. "I'd like to know, too."

He swallowed hard, then shrugged. "I got mad, I guess."

"Mad?" asked Keane. "Mad at whom?"

"At you guys, for being mad at each other. I didn't want what happened to you and Mom to happen to you and Gypsy, and . . . I got mad."

Gypsy felt Keane's regret even as he lifted his eyes to her. She had regrets of her own. Why did it take someone Kevin's age to show two adults that they were acting like children? "Well," she said cheerfully. "I don't know about you two, but I'm anxious to get out of here."

"We've got a flat, remember?" Keane reminded her.

"All the more reason for me to get on the radio and tell Neal to have someone come get us."

"You've got your plane out there?" Kevin asked.

"Sure do."

"Can I, like, sit in it or something?"

Gypsy pretended to consider. "I suppose so, if your father says it's all right."

"Dad?"

Keane stood. Even if Kevin was able to forgive and forget that quickly, it was clear he couldn't. "You and I have some serious talking ahead of us, Kev, I want you to know that. Go and look at the plane. Just remember it's not over between us."

"Yes, sir," he mumbled, then turned to leave the barn.

"One more thing," Keane called after him. "How did you manage to find this place, anyway?"

Kevin faced him with an expression he'd probably never shown him before. "The bus was heading west when it broke down, so I kept heading west. This was the first place I came to. I thought you guys would've been able to figure that out." He fished around in his pocket and pulled out a compass. "See? Magnetic west."

Keane stared at him. "Right. How thoughtless of us." When the boy was out of earshot, he turned to Gypsy. "Suddenly I feel like I don't know him at all. I mean, how do I treat him from here on in?"

"The way you always have," she told him. "Like

a father. Do you honestly think he wants that to change?"

"I don't know." He took her arm and began to walk out with her, back into the sunlight. "So much has happened, so fast, it's a wonder I can keep anything straight. *I'm* no genius."

She smiled. "I never said I wanted a genius."

He remained quiet for a time, till they were halfway to the Moth, then he slowed to a halt. "What exactly made you decide to land here?"

She thought about it for the first time. "I'm not sure, really. I guess it seemed like too much of a coincidence to ignore. This barn, the dreams—"

"I know," he agreed. "Scary, isn't it? We even dream alike. I wish we could work that well together when we're awake."

A gentle breeze began to blow, ruffling his hair, and Gypsy thought back to other words they'd said, at other times.

"I must be out of my mind."
"Come on, my company can't be that bad."

"We've got something special here, and we want it to go forward. Right or wrong?"
"Right."

"Bet you gave up on me, didn't you?"
"Me, give up? Don't be ridiculous."

"Would it be . . . that impossible?" she wondered aloud.

He shook his head and chuckled. "If you're asking me what kind of future we might expect, I haven't got a clue. But it would be interesting to find out, wouldn't it?"

"Don't quote me on this, but you have got a point there."

"Besides," he said, moving closer to her, "you have to admit, life would be pretty dull without me around to argue with."

She caught her breath as he lifted her chin. "Another good point."

"I knew you'd see the light," he whispered just before he brought his lips to hers in a featherlight kiss.

"You do have a certain . . . persuasive way about you," she said when she was able.

"Then you're really willing to give us a try, long term?"

"I am if you are."

"Ah, spoken like a true romantic."

"Then how's this? I love you."

"Hmm, simple but direct. Yeah, I think that'll do."

"Come on, you guys!" Kevin called from the Moth. "I've got Neal on the radio!"

Gypsy smiled. "He's got Neal on the radio."

"Then by all means." Keane laughed as they began to walk again. "Let's get this show on the road. Or should I say, in the air."

From the <u>New York Times</u> bestselling author
of <u>Morning Glory</u>

LaVyrle Spencer

One of today's best-loved authors
of bittersweet human drama and
captivating romance.

___SPRING FANCY (On sale Sept. '89)	0-515-10122-2/$3.95
___YEARS	0-515-08489-1/$4.95
___SEPARATE BEDS	0-515-09037-9/$4.95
___HUMMINGBIRD	0-515-09160-X/$4.50
___A HEART SPEAKS	0-515-09039-5/$4.50
___THE GAMBLE	0-515-08901-X/$4.95
___VOWS	0-515-09477-3/$4.95
___THE HELLION	0-515-09951-1/$4.50